Eliza has thought of James as a faithful friend, but he sees her as much more.

James grinned and then became serious. "Eliza, I enjoyed this evening very much. So much that I hate to see it end." He searched her face. "Would you consider going with me next Saturday to see my farm? I'd really like to show it to you."

She smiled up at him. "Do I have to walk?"

He laughed. "I don't know. Do you think your father would loan me his buggy?"

"I don't imagine he'll say much against it. If he does, I might put in a good word for you."

James stepped closer, his hands on each of her elbows. "Does that mean you'll go?"

She nodded, unable to speak with him so near.

He leaned toward her. "Eliza, may I kiss you good night?"

Her heartbeat drummed in her ears. Without a word, she nodded.

As he pulled her into his arms and his lips lowered over hers, moisture came unbidden to her eyes. She had not expected such strong feelings to come with a simple kiss.

James smiled down at her. "You'd better go in before your father comes out."

Eliza walked into the house in a daze.

MILDRED COLVIN is a native Missourian with three children, one son-in-law, and two grandchildren. She and her husband have spent most of their married life providing a home for foster children, but now enjoy baby-sitting the grandchildren. Mildred writes inspirational romance because in the stories the truth of God's presence, even in the midst of trouble, can be portrayed. Her desire is to continue writing stories that uplift and encourage.

Books by Mildred Colvin

HEARTSONG PRESENTS
HP435—Circle of Vengeance – as M.J. Conner
HP543—Cora

Eliza

Mildred Colvin

Heartsong Presents

To my sister Jean Norval for her untiring help, making suggestions, solving problems, editing and polishing. Without her input, I would still be struggling with stacks of unreadable manuscripts.

To my sister Pat Willis for reading Eliza *twice—first to voice her concerns and then to okay the changes.*

Also, to my daughter Becka del Valle who delights in finding and deleting unnecessary words. Plotting is a joy with your input, Becka.

Thanks so much Becka, Pat, and Jean.

A note from the Author:
I love to hear from my readers! You may correspond with me by writing:

> **Mildred Colvin**
> **Author Relations**
> **PO Box 719**
> **Uhrichsville, OH 44683**

ISBN 1-59310-116-3

ELIZA

All Scripture quotations are taken from the King James Version of the Bible.

Our mission is to publish and distribute inspirational products offering exceptional value and biblical encouragement to the masses.

PRINTED IN THE U.S.A.

one

October 1836

"Do you think Lenny will be all right?" Eliza looked back at the small frame schoolhouse as if she could see her ten-year-old brother inside.

"I wouldn't worry about Lenny." Her father slowed his steps to match hers.

The early October sun felt warm on Eliza's back as they turned down South Street toward the business square in Springfield, Missouri. "I suppose you're right. It's just that Mother always taught him."

Father laughed. "Lenny can take care of himself."

Eliza sighed. "I suppose."

Although her mother had been gone more than a year, the pain of her passing remained with Eliza. She missed her gentle ways and the love she had shown to each of her six children. Eliza thought of Nora, her baby sister, and a smile touched her lips. Nora's birth had weakened their mother and indirectly caused her death, but the sweet baby had brought so much love and happiness into their lives as well, and Eliza missed her.

Nora lived sixty miles north in the country with their oldest sister, Vickie. Eliza longed for the day when they could return to their old home and bring Nora to Springfield. She held to Father's promise that as soon as they were settled here, they would go after Nora.

A freight wagon rumbled by. They stepped up on a low boardwalk leading past a large, two-story shop. The sign over the door read LEACH'S GENERAL STORE.

Eliza's father waved across the square to a man coming

from the bank building. He smiled and nodded at two women hurrying past on their way to the general store.

Eliza said, "Springfield is smaller than Saint Louis, but after living in the wilderness it seems large."

Her father smiled and nodded. "Three hundred inhabitants and growing."

They approached a small white building sandwiched between a millinery shop on one side and a larger empty building on the corner. A sign over the door read CHANDLER SHOP, ORVAL JACKSON, PROPRIETOR.

Eliza stepped inside, and the familiar odor of tallow assailed her senses.

Father watched her sniff the air. "There's nothing like the smell of a candle shop, is there?"

Eliza wrinkled her nose. "I can think of things that smell better."

He laughed. "Wait until nearer Christmas when I start using bayberry. You girls always liked it."

Eliza thought of her sister just older than herself. "I think Cora liked it best. I wish we could send her a bayberry candle for Christmas."

Father nodded. "But with no delivery service to our old backwoods home, she'll have to do without."

"I guess." Eliza ran her hand over the shiny dark oak counter that stood along one wall. Tall, slender candles lay on one end of it, sorted by size. Other candles hung by the wick from hooks on the walls and ceiling. Shelves along one wall held sconces, candleholders, lanterns, and snuffers. In one corner was a pile of cotton yarn waiting to be made into wicks. Sitting around the room were several candle stands made of walnut, cherry, oak, and the less expensive, pine. On top of each was a candle in a tall, brass candlestick.

Her father moved about, lighting the candles on the stands until a soft, warm glow filled the dark shop.

Eliza watched her father. "I guess it's time for me to go home and clean house."

"You can stay all day if you want, but I need to get to work. I've got an order to get out for Mrs. Wingate."

"Who's that? Someone important?"

"Her husband helped finance my business. His bank's across the street."

Eliza glanced toward the window as the front door opened. A young man stepped into the shop. "Mr. Jackson?"

"Yes, may I help you?"

The young man's gaze met Eliza's for just a moment before he turned his full attention to her father. "I'm James Hurley. Mrs. Wingate sent me. She said you were thinking of adding a cooperage and would be needing help."

"Of course." Father stepped forward, and the men shook hands. "I'm glad you stopped by." He nodded toward Eliza. "This is my daughter Eliza."

James acknowledged her presence with a slight bow. "Mrs. Wingate mentioned that you and your brother would be arriving in town soon. I'm glad to meet you."

Eliza smiled at him. "We came in last night. I was just on my way home. I'll see you later, Father. For dinner?"

Her father nodded. "I'll pick Lenny up, and we'll be at the house about noon."

"All right." Eliza closed the door behind her and started across the square toward home. So her father was already adding on and would be hiring an employee. Perhaps the challenge of starting a new business was what he needed to heal his grieving heart from her mother's death.

She turned up the path to a large, two-story house set back from the road on the outskirts of town. She knew her father had bought the house by using most of his savings from some investments he had made years ago when they lived in St. Louis. The house had come completely furnished because the woman who had lived in it couldn't tolerate the frontier existence of Springfield. Eliza smiled as she wondered what the woman would have thought of the log cabin they had just moved from. Their nearest neighbor had been almost two miles away.

She let herself in, and an hour later she had fluffy mashed potatoes, fried pork, a pan of corn bread, and a bowl of left-over brown beans sitting on the table. She stood back and studied her work. Father liked fruit with his noon meal.

She looked around the well-ordered kitchen. Was there a pantry? When they'd come the evening before, she hadn't explored the house so she didn't know what treasures it held.

She opened the back door and went through a small ante-room lined with tools and a bin of firewood to the outdoors.

A long, white wooden door lay at an angle from the ground to the upper foundation of the house. She lifted the door, leaning it against the outside of the anteroom. Musty dampness filled her nostrils as she descended the steps. She stood at the bottom to light the candle she had brought.

The back door slammed. "Eliza, where are you?"

"Down here, Father." She turned, glad to run back up the steps to the bright, sunlit yard. "I thought there might be some fruit in the cellar."

"Well, what are we waiting for? Let's see if we can find a jar of peaches."

A flurry from behind him brought Lenny to the front. "I want to go, too."

"Great, you can keep the mice and bats away." Eliza grasped each of Lenny's shoulders and held him in front of her. "How was school this morning?"

"Aw, it was all right." He swiped at a spiderweb.

"Look at this." Father's voice brought her attention back to the cellar. "Mr. Wingate said it was fully stocked, but I didn't expect to find a cellar full of food."

"Father, you've been here more than two months. Haven't you even looked down here? How have you been eating?" Eliza looked from the full shelves to her father.

In the soft light of the candle, Father's grin looked sheepish. "There's a café in town for men like me who can't feed themselves."

Eliza took a jar of peaches off the shelf. "Well, you won't

need to go there anymore." She left the cellar, calling over her shoulder. "Come on, our meal is getting cold."

※

The next morning Eliza woke to a thick blanket of clouds and drizzling rain. The rain stopped midmorning, and by the time she had the noon dishes cleaned and put away, she felt she had been confined to the house long enough. About an hour after her father and brother left, she grabbed her shawl and headed out the door for town.

She hummed a hymn as her feet covered the damp ground. Not until she saw her father's shop did she slow her gait. There had been no real reason to come to town. As far as she knew, the house was well stocked. She didn't need to see her father about anything. Yet she would have to pass by his shop to reach the general store. Without a doubt he would see her and welcome the chance to tease her about neglecting her duties. She giggled. She wouldn't give him a chance. She'd tell him the clouds made it so dark inside she needed more candles.

Eliza pulled open the door and stepped inside. "Father, you wouldn't believe how dark it gets when the sun doesn't shine."

The man behind the counter was not her father. She knew it before he turned and looked at her with those clear, gray eyes that she remembered from the day before when James Hurley had first stepped into her father's shop. A slow smile lit James's face. His voice held a deep timbre, smooth and, resonant. "Yes, but if the sun shone all the time, we'd sell very few candles."

Eliza glanced toward the back room. "Where is my father?"

"He stepped out for a few minutes."

"And left you here alone?" As soon as the words were out of her mouth, she wished she could call them back.

One eyebrow lifted as James pinned her with a glare. "I don't plan to steal the profits, Miss Jackson."

A flush spread over Eliza's face. "I'm sorry. I didn't mean that. I just meant it's only your second day on the job."

"Actually, it's my first." James grinned. "I'm a quick study. At least your father seems to trust me enough to leave me alone for ten minutes."

"Oh." Eliza had never found it hard to talk to anyone before. But there was something about those gray eyes looking at her and the way James smiled that made her want to leave and stay at the same time. She decided it would be best if she left when memories she had thought long buried rose in her mind.

Ralph Stark, a young man from her old home, had smiled at her in much the same way. When Ralph had looked at her with that same intense gleam in his eyes, she had felt special and pretty. She had loved him and thought he loved her. Then, during their courtship, he'd married someone else, leaving her with the pain of rejection. Strength gained through her newfound relationship with the Lord had brought her through that time, yet she wondered even now if she would ever forget her first sweetheart.

The cool, damp air felt good on her hot cheeks as she turned back toward home. Her appetite for browsing through the general store had been squelched.

When Thursday morning dawned clear, Eliza decided it was time to wash clothes while she could hang them on the line. She worked hard all morning, barely finding time to fix the noon meal for her father and brother.

But she soon had stew simmering on the stove and was throwing the potato peelings into the slop bucket when she heard steps at the door. Moments later, Lenny ran into the kitchen.

"Look what I got this morning." He strutted up to her and lifted his face.

Dried blood lined one nostril. He squinted at her through his red, swollen left eye. Eliza looked toward the doorway where her father lounged against the frame.

He shrugged. "Ask him what happened."

She turned back to her little brother, her hands folded

across her chest. "Well, are you going to tell me?"

"Ah, Eliza, it ain't nothin' to get upset about." Lenny looked pleased with himself. "It was just a little old fight."

Her father spoke proudly from the doorway. "If you think he looks bad, you should've seen the other fellow."

Eliza turned toward her father. How could he condone this?

He laughed. "Don't look at me that way. It was all over by the time I got there."

"Lenny, why did you get into a fight?" Eliza asked.

"'Cause I ain't no teacher's pet."

"You're not the teacher's pet," Eliza corrected.

"Right, I ain't." He touched his eye tenderly. "Cletis sure can hit hard."

"Cletis?"

Lenny nodded. "Yeah. Cletis Hall. Can he come over sometime?"

"Here? To our house?" Eliza couldn't believe him. "Why do you want him to come here? I thought you just had a fight with him."

"Your sister doesn't understand a man's way of doing things, Lenny." Father pulled out a chair. He looked at Eliza. "You see, Cletis didn't have any respect for the teacher's pet, but he's got a lot of respect for the first boy in school who was brave enough to whip him."

Eliza could hear pride in her father's voice. She looked from him to Lenny. "So you made a friend by beating him up?" She shook her head. "You're right. I don't understand it. Bring your friend here to play if you want. Just make sure he doesn't mess my house up. And there'd better not be any more fighting."

Lenny grinned and as quickly grimaced. Father stood. "Come on, Lenny. Let's take care of that eye."

Eliza watched them go and shook her head. She reached for the long-handled spoon to stir her stew. She didn't need to worry about Lenny. Obviously, he could take care of himself.

two

Eliza tilted the coffee canister and looked inside. Less than half full. She wanted to see what Leach's General Store had in stock, and this was as good an excuse as any.

She ran upstairs to change into her afternoon visiting dress. The black-and-pink-striped silk was terribly out of date, but she had nothing better. She shrugged, reaching for the matching silk bonnet. She went downstairs and out the front door, determined to enjoy her afternoon. Only this time she would avoid the chandler shop and James Hurley.

Red and yellow leaves, blending with the green of the trees overhead, provided a colorful canopy for her walk. In the distance a dog barked and another answered. Smoke from a backyard fire wafted by, teasing her nose as she passed a house.

She reached the business square a few minutes later. She tried to hurry past her father's shop, but before she reached the door, two women came out, each clutching a package.

"Thank you, and please come again." James smiled at the women as he held the door for them.

Eliza looked up and caught his gaze on her. She smiled. "Hello, Mr. Hurley. I see my father is keeping you busy."

He grinned. "Good afternoon, Miss Jackson. Could I interest you in candles, a new cherry candle stand, or maybe a snuffer?"

"No, thank you. I'm on my way to the general store."

"Ah, Mr. Leach's gain is our loss."

She smiled as she went on. Maybe her father's new employee was just being friendly when he smiled at her.

It took a moment for her eyes to adjust to the dim interior of the store. A potbellied stove held center stage with an open cracker barrel nearby. Elderly men took from its contents while they argued politics.

The aromas of tobacco, leather, and fresh ground coffee

mingled with the familiar smell of the wood-burning stove. She hesitated a moment as she looked around. Mr. Leach must have the best stocked store in town, with not an inch of space wasted. Everything from Bibles to medicine, coal oil to calico, and school supplies to candy had its own special place. A wide assortment of hardware, household goods, and groceries filled the shelves.

Eliza's heels clicked on the wooden floor as she moved down the center aisle past the grocery counter and dry goods shelves. Mr. Leach, busy behind his high counter in the back, greeted her with a warm smile. "Good afternoon. What can I do for you?"

Eliza smiled. "I need a pound of coffee."

"Then a pound of coffee you shall have." The storekeeper nodded toward one side of the store. "Have yourself a look around while I get it. We just got in some new calico the other day."

Eliza turned and wound her way past kegs and barrels of flour, sugar, vinegar, and molasses. Close to a half hour later, oblivious to the activity around her, Eliza picked up the corner of a blue-sprigged calico and rubbed it between her fingers. How she wished she could sew decently! But no matter how often her mother or her sisters, Vickie and Cora, had tried to teach her, she could never force her fingers to take the tiny stitches needed for dressmaking.

"Are you finding anything you like?" Eliza turned to see a middle-aged woman, her plump face wreathed with a friendly smile.

Eliza sighed. "Oh, there are so many, and I like all of them." She refolded the calico and turned away. "But I came for coffee, not fabric."

"A young girl can always use a new dress." The woman eyed Eliza's outdated frock. She extended her hand. "I'm Alice Leach, the storekeeper's wife."

Eliza placed her hand in the woman's strong grasp. "I'm glad to meet you. I'm Eliza Jackson. My father recently opened the chandler shop down the street."

"Oh, yes. Mr. Leach was telling me that the chandler's family had arrived. Welcome to Springfield."

Eliza nodded. "I guess I should be starting home. I'm sure your husband has my coffee ready by now."

"Come back anytime. Next time you need a new dress, let me know, and we'll find you something pretty."

Eliza took the coffee and turned to leave as another customer came in. She watched the girl breeze through the store to the high counter where Mr. Leach stood.

"Hello, Miss Vanda," Mr. Leach greeted her. "What can I do for you today?"

Eliza slipped out the door as the other girl gave her order. Vanda. What an unusual name. It was pretty, just as the girl was.

Eliza crossed the square and turned north on the road leading home. Dust swirled about her skirt as she hurried. She had spent most of the afternoon accomplishing nothing. She'd better be thinking of supper.

She set her package of coffee on the table in the kitchen and then went upstairs to change clothes. She had no sooner taken her bonnet and wraps off than a knock on the door downstairs startled her.

With her heart pounding, she ran downstairs and opened the door, surprised to see the girl from the store.

"Hello. Won't you come in?" Eliza smiled and stepped back.

Vanda stood unmoved. "Is your mother home?"

Eliza's heart constricted at the question. She shook her head. "My mother died a year ago."

"Your father isn't here, is he?" An uncertain expression crossed the girl's face.

Eliza shook her head. "No, he's at work."

"Then you are the only one home?"

"Yes, won't you come in?" Eliza repeated the invitation.

Vanda walked to the middle of the room and looked around. Her eyes rested briefly on the covered sofa with gleaming mahogany legs and two matching chairs. Her gaze swept past the fireplace, then dropped to the carpet before she turned to Eliza.

"Won't you sit down?" Eliza could scarcely believe she had company.

Vanda looked at the sofa but shook her head. "No, what I've got to say won't take long."

"Oh." Eliza wondered at the sharp tone in the girl's voice.

"You have a brother named Lenny, don't you?" Vanda's eyes bore into hers.

Eliza nodded. Surely Lenny couldn't have done anything to Vanda.

"Is he about nine or ten years old?" Vanda's hands were on her hips now.

"He's ten." Eliza was puzzled. "He's been in school all week, except at night when he's been home. We just moved in last week."

"I have a ten-year-old brother, too. Maybe you've heard of him." Vanda paused. "Cletis Von Hall."

"Cletis Von Hall?" Eliza repeated the name. She frowned, trying to remember. Lenny had said the boy he fought was Cletis Hall.

Eliza met the other girl's gaze. "Yes, Lenny told us about the fight he had with Cletis. He also said he and Cletis are now good friends."

"Good friends!" Vanda's eyes widened. "Good friends don't give each other black eyes."

"Oh, I don't think they were friends when they fought." Eliza wasn't sure she could explain what she didn't understand herself. "You see, the fight itself is what made them friends."

A sneer crossed Vanda's face. "My little brother was beaten black and blue, and you tell me he's friends with the boy who did it?"

"I know it doesn't make sense, but that's what Lenny said."

"It certainly doesn't make sense, and I don't want it to happen again." Vanda took a step forward, her forefinger lifted toward Eliza. "Either you see to it, or my father will."

Eliza watched the angry girl step to the door.

"I'm sorry Lenny hurt your brother." Eliza followed her out. "I'll speak to him about it."

Vanda paid no attention to Eliza. She stood on the porch, her hand resting on a post.

Eliza looked over her shoulder to see what had caught her attention. Coming up the road arm in arm was Lenny with another boy.

"Cletis Elliot Von Hall!" Vanda's exclamation brought the boys up short. "What on earth are you doing?"

The boy shook a heavy lock of blond hair off his forehead. "I ain't doin' nothin' wrong."

"What are you doing with. . .him?"

Cletis frowned at his sister. "Me and Lenny's buddies."

Cletis had gotten the worst of the fight. Both of his eyes were blackened. His lower lip had swelled, and a bruise marred his cheekbone.

The two boys stood in front of Vanda. Cletis looked up at her. "Ah, Sis, you ain't gonna make a big thing out of that old fight, are you?"

Vanda stood, her arms crossed, looking at her brother. Finally, she spoke. "Do you mean you let some boy beat you up, and then you made friends with him?"

Cletis waved his hand at her. "Don't worry, Sis. This is men stuff."

Vanda made an exasperated sound and turned to Eliza. "He got that from my older brother and my father. Every time they do something stupid, that's what they say. Sometimes I get so mad I could bite a nail."

Eliza smiled. "I had the same conversation with Lenny and my father last night. They told me I wouldn't understand."

For the first time since they met, Vanda's expression softened. "I'm sorry for the way I stormed into your house and for the things I said."

Eliza shook her head. "Don't be. You were only protecting your little brother. I'd have done the same."

Vanda held her hand out. "I'm Vanda Von Hall. I don't know your first name."

Eliza smiled and grasped her hand. "Eliza."

Vanda shook her hand. "I guess I'd better be getting

home." She picked up her bundle of purchases. "I need to get supper before my father gets there."

Eliza laughed. "It sounds like you have the same job I do. My father will be home before long, too, and I haven't even decided what to fix."

She turned to Lenny. "Does Father know you came home from school without him?"

Lenny nodded. "Sure. We went by the shop, and he said it was all right."

"He was probably glad to get Cletis out of his shop."

Eliza laughed at Vanda's cryptic remark.

"Can I stay and play with Lenny?" Cletis looked at his sister.

"No, you'd better be home when Poppa gets there."

Cletis kicked at a rock and mumbled.

Vanda shook her head when Cletis shuffled away. "I'm so sorry. Sometimes Cletis gets out of hand, and my temper does, too. It's hard without a mother, but I guess you know that. Mine's been gone two years now."

"I'm sorry. About your mother, I mean." Eliza laid her hand on the other girl's arm. "I'm glad I got to meet you. When you have time, come back and visit. I get lonesome with just my father and brother."

"I know." Vanda smiled. "I've got to go." She walked away, calling over her shoulder, "I'll be back, I promise."

Eliza watched as Vanda grabbed her little brother's arm and pulled him down the road. When they reached the corner, they both waved. Eliza and Lenny stood on the porch waving until their new friends turned the corner and were lost to sight.

Eliza woke early Sunday morning. She hurried through a breakfast of biscuits and oatmeal before getting ready for church.

Three hours later, Eliza sat at the end of the pew beside Lenny. She had hoped the Von Halls would be at church. But she saw neither Vanda nor Cletis.

As she turned her attention back to the sermon, the eerie feeling of someone staring at her crept up her backbone. She turned to meet the scrutiny of James Hurley. His gray eyes locked with her brown ones for only seconds before she turned away.

Eliza tried to pay attention to the sermon, but her mind wandered up and down the pews. There were several young people near her own age. Would they accept her? Would they become her friends?

She sighed, forcing herself to listen to the remainder of the sermon. When the last "amen" had been said, people began to stir. Eliza stood and stepped out into the aisle ahead of Lenny and Father. They made their way to the back door, nodding and speaking to everyone they saw.

Finally, they reached the minister. "We're so glad to see you again this morning, Mr. Jackson." He clasped Father's hand and gave it a hearty shake. "I haven't had the privilege of meeting your children."

As Father introduced them, Eliza saw James Hurley help a woman, who she assumed was his mother, into a farm wagon while a young girl climbed in the back.

The pastor smiled at Eliza. "We've got a good group of young people here. It won't be long until you have many friends."

"Thank you, Sir." She smiled. "I hope you're right."

As he turned to Lenny, she looked back toward the road and saw James climb in beside his mother. He picked up the reins, then looked at her and smiled.

Her breath caught in her throat. With a flick of the reins, the wagon moved out. Eliza watched until he turned the corner and drove out of sight.

"Mr. and Mrs. Wingate, so good to see you." The pastor's voice brought Eliza's attention to a fashionably attired, middle-aged couple stepping out of the church.

"Good sermon, Pastor. Just what we needed this morning." Mr. Wingate put a tall-crowned, brushed-beaver hat on his head. He stepped off the porch and shook her father's hand. "How's that chandler shop, Orval?"

Eliza moved with her father and the Wingates a short distance from the church. Lenny ran off to play with some other boys.

"Considering the condition of our pocketbooks at this

time, not bad." Father smiled at Mrs. Wingate. "I appreciate your business and the customers you've sent."

Mrs. Wingate, a tall, blond woman smiled. "I recognize quality when I see it. I would never go back to making my own candles."

Eliza couldn't visualize the woman before her bent over a vat of foul smelling tallow.

"Have you thought more about adding a cooperage?" Mrs. Wingate asked.

"Actually, yes." Father nodded. "I took your advice and hired the young man you sent. We've been working on getting the building next door ready. James is a good worker."

"Excellent." Mrs. Wingate looked pleased. "I thought he would be."

She turned to Eliza. "You must be Mr. Jackson's daughter Eliza."

Eliza nodded. "I'm pleased to meet you, Mrs. Wingate." She felt dowdy compared to the well-dressed woman before her. In the country, it hadn't mattered, but here she felt keenly the difference between her dress and the clothing worn around her.

The woman linked her arm in Eliza's. "I'm so glad you've come to Springfield to live. We've enjoyed having your father here, and I know you and your brother will become dear to us as well." She didn't wait for a response but asked, "Have you met my son Charles?"

Eliza shook her head. "No, I've been here only a week and haven't met anyone." She thought of Vanda and added, "Except one girl."

"Oh? Who might that be?" A spark of interest shone from the woman's eyes as she centered her attention on Eliza.

"Her name is Vanda Von Hall. I thought she might be at church this morning, but I didn't see her."

"No, she wasn't here today." Mrs. Wingate frowned. "Her older brother, Trennen, is our driver. I've often wondered if we should have him drive us to church on Sundays just to get him here."

She smiled then. "How do you like living in Springfield?"

"It's very nice. I love the house Father bought."

Mrs. Wingate nodded. "Yes, it is a nice place. You were very fortunate to get it." She paused a moment before asking, "It must be hard trying to keep up with that large house and an active brother, too."

"Oh, no." Eliza shook her head. "I enjoy my work."

"But a young girl needs to get out and play once in awhile. Maybe your father will remarry someday, and you'll be free to pursue other interests."

Eliza had been close to her mother. She could never imagine another woman taking her place. She shook her head; her voice lowered. "No, I don't expect my father to ever marry again. I don't mind taking care of the house. He doesn't need a wife."

Eliza recognized the calculating look in Mrs. Wingate's blue eyes as she nodded. "I'm sure you do a wonderful job, Dear. My husband claims my worst fault is interfering." She glanced toward her husband and smiled. "Speaking of Mr. Wingate, I believe he's ready to leave." She patted Eliza's arm. "I'm glad we got to visit. You come see me sometime, all right?"

At Eliza's nod, the older woman turned away. Eliza collected Lenny, and they left, too.

"Winter will soon be here," Father commented as they walked home.

"Yes, that's true." When the snow and cold weather moved into the area, Eliza knew she would be confined to the house. She didn't look forward to that time.

"Seems someone is having a birthday before long." Father smiled at her.

"Is that right?" Eliza fell into his joking mood. "Are you going to get that person something nice?"

Father laughed. "Sounds like you know whose birthday is coming up."

Eliza laughed with her father. She was well aware that she would soon be nineteen. Plenty old enough to run a motherless household.

three

A week later, Father opened his cooperage in the building next to the chandler shop. Unlike the shops in St. Louis he had shared with his brother, there was no door connecting the two buildings, so he rigged a string and bell from one shop's door to the other. When either door opened, the bells would ring in both shops. It wasn't a perfect system, but it let Father and James know when they had a customer.

After working both shops for two days, Father came home exhausted. Eliza found him sprawled across the sofa after supper. Lenny lay on his stomach on the floor, reading a book.

She touched her father's shoulder. "I know it's early, but if you want to go to bed, I'll see that Lenny settles down at his bedtime."

"What would I do without you, Eliza?" Father pulled himself up. "I wouldn't be so tired except for running back and forth between those two shops."

"Can't you move them both into the same building?"

He shook his head. "No. Neither place is big enough. What I need is another person to run the candle shop until I get James trained."

"Is he having trouble learning?"

Father shook his head. "No. He's doing fine. It's just that there's so much to learn. I want him to learn the chandler trade as well. That way I can trust either shop to him if necessary."

"Father." An idea took shape in Eliza's mind. "Could I take care of the chandler shop?"

Father stared at her. Eliza's heart beat fast against her ribs. A log in the fireplace snapped, sending sparks into the room. They both rushed to step on them, crushing them out before they burned through the rug.

21

Father returned to the sofa. When he finally spoke, his expression was solemn. "For two weeks in the afternoon only."

"You mean I can?"

Father laughed. "You'd think I just gave you a gift." He patted the sofa. "Sit down here and let me tell you what you're getting into."

As Eliza listened to her father explain her new duties, she tingled with excitement. Finally, she would be in the hub of the town's activities. Every afternoon for two weeks she could visit with the women and girls who came into Father's shop.

Eliza's excitement continued into the next morning as she hurried through her chores. She heard a knock on the door downstairs just as she smoothed the covers on Lenny's bed.

"Oh, no." She groaned. "I have little enough time without someone calling." She smoothed her hair and ran down the stairs.

She opened the door to Vanda's smile. Eliza stepped back. "Please, come in."

"I intended to come sooner, but I've been busy." Vanda's gaze swept the room. "You have such a nice house."

"Thank you. We really like it." Eliza closed the door. "Won't you sit down?"

As Vanda sat on the sofa, Eliza took the chair and leaned forward, eager to share her news. "Oh, Vanda, you'll never guess what I'm going to do this afternoon."

Vanda relaxed back into the sofa. "What?"

"I'm going to work in my father's shop." Eliza's light brown eyes sparkled.

"When do you start?"

"Right after noon."

"Oh, then I'm probably keeping you." Vanda stood.

Eliza knew she should finish her work, but she and Vanda hadn't had a chance to talk. She shook her head. "All I have left to do is prepare dinner. That shouldn't take long."

"What are you fixing?"

"I've had beans on the back of the stove since early this

morning. I need to bake corn bread and fry some meat."

Vanda nodded. "How long until your father comes?"

Eliza looked at the clock sitting on the mantel. "Almost an hour."

"Let me help," Vanda pleaded. "I'll leave before he gets here. He needn't ever know I was here."

"That won't be necessary." Eliza frowned. "I mean, you don't have to help. Just stay and visit with me. Why don't you stay for dinner?"

"Oh, I couldn't do that."

"Is your father expecting you?"

Vanda shook her head. "No, Poppa's gone all this week. He's working at a sawmill east of here."

"Then there's no one to worry about you, unless your brothers. . . ?"

"No, Cletis takes his lunch, and Trennen eats at the Wingates'."

Eliza took her arm. "Good, then it's settled. Let's go to the kitchen while we talk."

She led the way, and they were soon visiting like old friends. Vanda insisted on mixing the corn bread while Eliza fried meat and set the table.

When Eliza set four plates out, Vanda looked at her. "Are you sure your father won't mind?"

Eliza laughed. "He'll be glad I've found a friend."

Vanda pulled the golden-brown corn bread from the oven just as Father stepped through the kitchen doorway. His hazel eyes twinkled. "Well, what have we here?" He turned to Lenny, who had come in behind him. "You put a woman to work outside the home, and the first thing she does is get help with her household chores."

Lenny stepped around his father. "Are you going to be our housekeeper?"

Vanda's cheeks flamed as she looked at Eliza. Eliza took Lenny's shoulder and pushed him toward the sink. "Go wash your hands. You know Cletis's sister. She's our guest."

Father ran his hand over his hair. He smiled at Vanda. "I'm sorry. I sometimes get carried away teasing my daughter. I'm glad you're here with Eliza. Please, make yourself at home."

After that they enjoyed an uneventful dinner hour until time to go back to work and school. Eliza rushed through the dishwashing with Vanda's help. As they put the last dish away, Vanda glanced toward the door leading to the parlor.

"Your father seems nice. Is he always like that?"

Eliza made a face. "Actually, he was on his best behavior. The way he acted when he first came in is more like his true self. He's terribly fond of teasing."

"That's because he loves you."

"Yes, I know." Eliza started for the door. "What's your father like? Does he like to tease, too?"

A crease formed between Vanda's eyes as she frowned and followed Eliza. "No, Poppa doesn't tease. Especially not since Momma died."

"He must have loved her very much." Eliza picked up her cape as they passed through the parlor. Father and Lenny had gone ahead so the two girls would be walking by themselves.

Vanda shrugged. "I suppose." She followed Eliza out the front door and waited while she closed it.

A touch of dampness clung to the air under a canopy of gray clouds. Eliza pulled her cape close, glad for its warmth. She glanced at her friend, realizing for the first time that Vanda's clothing was as outdated as her own.

Several minutes later the two girls stopped in front of the chandler shop. After saying good-bye to Vanda and promising they'd get together soon, Eliza went inside. She didn't see her father in the store so she looked in the back room. No sign of him there, either. She stood in the doorway and looked at the disarray that made up his workroom. He and Lenny had left the house several minutes before she and Vanda. Where was he?

❧

James glanced out the front window of the cooperage and saw Eliza go past with Vanda Von Hall. He stepped closer to the window. They stopped in front of the chandler shop and talked a moment before Vanda moved on. Eliza went into the shop, setting off the bells that were rigged to ring if either shop door opened. James ignored the ringing bell and turned back to his work. He didn't have time to stare at a girl when he had barrels to make.

The half-finished barrel he had been working on was the last of an order that needed to be delivered that afternoon. He'd better get it finished. He stepped over and around tools, metal rings, barrels, and tubs to the far wall where wood slats were stacked. He crouched down behind a large barrel to select the slats he needed from the pile on the floor.

The door opened with barely a jingle of the bell. James peered around the barrel and saw the blue of Eliza's skirt. His stomach turned somersaults as he watched her gaze sweep the large room. When she turned as if to leave, he stood up, afraid she would go and he wouldn't get to talk to her. In his haste, he bumped the large barrel in front of him, causing it to rock on its bottom. He grabbed a cloth to wipe his sweating palms and stepped out from the barrel.

Taking a couple of steps toward her, he asked, "May I help you, Ma'am?"

James couldn't keep the silly grin from his face when she turned back to face him, her eyes wide and beautiful.

"I'm looking for my father."

"Do you make a habit of misplacing him?" He couldn't resist teasing her.

"Oh, honestly!" She reached for the door.

Instantly contrite, James chuckled. "I'm sorry. He isn't back from dinner yet."

"I see. Have you eaten?"

James's smile grew wider. "Not yet. I'll eat when your father gets back. I brought my lunch. Thank you for thinking of me, though."

James admired the red that tinged Eliza's cheeks as she stammered, "I didn't. . .think. . .oh, that's all right."

As she jerked the outside door open and slipped out, he reached to stop her before he realized what he was doing. Eliza Jackson was his boss's daughter. He had no business teasing her or even thinking of her in a romantic way. Again, he turned back to work.

❧

Eliza hurried toward the chandler shop and almost bumped into her father.

"Well, have you been visiting with the new apprentice?" His eyes sparkled as they searched her red face.

"Father!" Eliza welcomed the cool breeze that floated by. "I was looking for you. I thought you'd be here by now since you left the house before I did."

Her father laughed as he opened the door to the chandler shop. "I stopped by the school. Lenny said his teacher wanted to talk to me."

Eliza stepped into the store ahead of her father. She turned quickly, her embarrassment forgotten. "What did he do?"

"Nothing." He chuckled. "She wants some of the fathers to build props for the school Christmas program."

"Christmas already?" Eliza gave him a skeptical look.

Her father laughed. "Yes, Christmas already. It's not a bad idea to get started early on the construction."

❧

After supper on Saturday, Father challenged Lenny to a game of checkers. He won the first game against Lenny, so Eliza played the second and also lost to him.

She set her pieces back on the squares. "Now it's time for the losers to play, Father. You may watch this game."

Father let Lenny take his chair and grinned at Eliza. "You think I can learn something from watching you two play?"

She nodded. "Certainly. If you watch closely enough, you can learn how to lose."

It wasn't long until Lenny jumped one of Eliza's pieces. She tried to concentrate on the game, but too much was on her mind. Finally, Lenny jumped her last piece. He sprang to his feet, twirling around. "I won. I won."

"Well, don't gloat about it." Eliza picked the game up and carried it across the room to the mantle.

Father laughed as Lenny fell down against him. "Eliza was right. I did pick up some pointers from her game."

Eliza tried to make a face at them, but it soon turned to a laugh. "All right, so I'm not a good checkers player." She sat in the chair opposite the one they shared. "Do you know what today is?"

Father nodded, his voice subdued. "Yes, it's Nora's second birthday." He pulled Lenny onto his lap. "She's old enough now to come home. As soon as we can, we'll bring our little girl here to live with us. I promise."

Eliza clung to his promise. She missed her little sister so much. Vickie had taken her right after their mother's funeral to care for along with her own son, Christopher, who was just a few months older. The arrangement should have been temporary, but the first few months had been hard as Father grieved for his wife. Then, Father gave his life to the Lord one day as his oldest son, Ben, prayed with him. After that, Father decided to move to Springfield, and the time never came to bring Nora home.

Father pushed Lenny from his lap. "Run and get my Bible. It's almost bedtime."

Father read a passage of Scripture and prayed. Then he stood, running his hand over his thinning hair. "I completely forgot. Lenny, your teacher said there'll be a spelling bee and social next Saturday night at the schoolhouse."

Lenny's eyes brightened. "Can we go? I bet I can outspell everyone in that school."

Father laughed. "In that case, we'll have to go and see. How about it, Eliza? Do you think you can outspell everyone in school?"

She smiled. "I don't know, but I'm willing to try if you are."

A wide grin set on Father's face. "I wouldn't miss it."

Eliza saw James Hurley come in to the crowded schoolhouse with his sister and mother. He smiled and spoke to her as he passed.

"I'm glad you came." Vanda took her arm. "Would you like to meet my poppa and Trennen? They're both here."

"Of course." Eliza followed her across the crowded room.

"Poppa, I'd like you to meet my friend."

"If you'll excuse me." Mr. Von Hall nodded to the men he had been talking with. He smiled at Eliza.

"Poppa, this is Eliza Jackson. She moved here a month ago with her father and brother."

"I'm pleased to meet you. I hope you'll like our town." Mr. Von Hall was a tall man with thick blond hair and blue eyes. He appeared warm and friendly. There was something about his carefree smile that reminded her of Ralph. Eliza decided that she liked him.

She smiled. "I already like Springfield very much."

"Poppa, where's Trennen? I want to introduce him to Eliza." Vanda searched the room and jumped when a masculine voice spoke behind her.

"Who are you wanting me to meet?"

Eliza turned with Vanda to see a tall, slim, dark-haired young man with an engaging smile. His gaze shifted from Vanda to Eliza as his sister started talking.

"Trennen, I want you to meet my friend, Eliza Jackson." Vanda smiled at Eliza. "This is my big brother, Trennen."

Eliza's smile froze as she met the blue eyes of Vanda's older brother. His look swept over her before resting on her face. Her heart thumped hard. Her lashes lowered. "Pleased to meet you."

She felt his hand close around her fingers as he lifted them for a quick handshake. "And I'm pleased to meet you."

Eliza noticed the personal tone of his voice. She pulled her fingers from his grasp and turned away, glad for Miss Fraser's shrill voice demanding attention.

"We're ready to start," the schoolmarm announced. "Please, let's have order."

The room grew quiet as all eyes turned toward the raised platform where Miss Fraser stood. "The children and I welcome you to our school for our annual community spelling bee. Everyone who wishes to compete, please form a line around the room. The rest are welcome to sit at the children's desks and watch. Thank you."

Again the hum of voices filled the room as everyone shuffled around, finding their places.

Eliza squeezed Vanda's hand. "You're going to spell, aren't you? I promised Father I would."

Vanda shrugged. "I might as well, I guess. But I'm not a good speller. I'll probably be put out the first word I get."

They were in line before Eliza realized that Trennen stood behind her. He cocked his eyebrows at her and smiled. "Good luck, Miss Jackson."

"Thank you." She tried hard to ignore his presence.

Miss Fraser stood behind her desk with a sheaf of papers lying before her. She raised her hand for silence and gave the first word to a small girl. "Miriam, give us the definition for the word *good* and then spell it, please."

One by one the words were given out, and the spelldown began. When either the definition or spelling was wrong, that person had to find an empty seat in the center. Several rounds later, the words grew in difficulty as the number of spellers diminished. One after another sat down when the word *stultiloquence* was given. Eliza knew it meant foolish talk, but she wasn't sure she could spell it. Surely someone would get it right before they reached her.

Vanda made a face, whispering, "Where'd she come up with that?"

Eliza shrugged and shook her head. "I don't know, but I hope someone spells it soon."

Her father was next. Eliza held her breath when the woman in front of him sat down.

Father said, "Stultiloquence means foolish talking, which I think has been established already." A ripple of laughter swept the room before he went on to correctly spell the word.

Eliza watched James step forward.

Miss Fraser looked up from her list. "Define and spell *serry*, please."

Eliza was aware of Trennen standing behind her, making occasional comments, obviously trying to hold her attention, and she compared the two. While James was at least three inches shorter than Trennen, he had a broader, more muscular frame. Trennen sported rakish good looks with his thick dark hair and expressive blue eyes. James, with gray eyes and light brown—almost blond—hair, was not as handsome, although he was far from homely.

Now he said, "*Serry* means to crowd and is spelled s-e-r-r-y."

Miss Fraser looked up and smiled. "It looks like our spelling is improving." She nodded toward James. "You may take your place at the end of the line."

As James passed Eliza, their gazes met and held for several seconds. He smiled and nodded.

Vanda missed the next word, passing it on to Eliza.

Miss Fraser smiled at her. "Miss Jackson, please define and spell *pulchritude.*"

Eliza took a breath to calm herself. "Pulchritude means beauty. P-u-l-c-h-r." She stopped. A vowel must come next, but was it *i* or *e?* She said the word to herself and guessed. "I-t-u-d-e."

Miss Fraser beamed at her. "That is correct. Please step to the end of the line."

Trennen stayed with her through the next round, and then left Eliza with six others, including her father and James. She listened to James define and spell *pneumonitis* without hesitation and decided Father had been right when he said James was intelligent.

One more round brought Eliza to the front with only four people behind her. She felt proud of staying in so long. Even

Father had taken a seat. She felt confident when Miss Fraser smiled at her and said, "Miss Jackson, your word is *timous*."

What an easy word! Eliza smiled. "Timous means timely. T-i-m-e-o-u-s."

"Oh, I'm sorry." Miss Fraser frowned.

Eliza's face burned as she took a seat with Vanda and Trennen. "I thought you'd never come sit by me." Vanda made light of Eliza's mistake.

Eliza sank into the seat, trying to compose herself. "I can't believe I did that. There's no *e* in timous. I must have had the word *time* on my mind."

"That's what it means." Trennen smiled at Eliza.

"Yes, but I knew better."

"Hey, you stayed in longer than I did." His easy grin soon had her feeling better.

Another competitor sat down. Vanda indicated the two remaining. "I wonder who will win—James Hurley or Mr. Stenson?"

"I don't know."

Miss Fraser threw out words that Eliza had never heard, and still the two men battled.

"This could go on forever." Vanda yawned.

Eliza nodded. "It certainly looks that way."

But it didn't. Whether he was tired or he really didn't know the word, when Miss Fraser called out *repudiation*, Mr. Stenson shook his head and frowned. "Don't reckon I know the meaning of that one." He looked up at Miss Fraser. "I could spell it though, I imagine."

"I'm sorry, but the definition must come first." Miss Fraser smiled. "Mr. Stenson, you've done a wonderful job of defining and spelling. Thank you."

Mr. Stenson nodded and stepped toward a nearby seat. Eliza watched James as he took a step forward and waited until Miss Fraser repeated the word. "Repudiation means rejection. R-e-p-u-d-i-a-t-i-o-n."

"That is correct." Miss Fraser shuffled her papers and laid

them neatly to one side while the room erupted in applause. She smiled at James. "Mr. Hurley, I'm certain I speak for everyone here when I say congratulations on an excellent evening of spelling. Will you please step forward?"

Eliza watched James step on the platform beside the schoolmarm's desk. He stuck both thumbs in his pockets and waited while she spoke.

"I want to congratulate all of our participants. However, a spelling bee may have only one winner. Some of our leading citizens decided that the winner of tonight's spelling bee deserved a prize. Mr. Wingate, on behalf of his bank, donated a half eagle that I am presenting to our 1836 spelling bee winner, Mr. James Hurley."

James took his right hand from his pocket. His neck was red as he reached for the five-dollar gold coin. He cleared his throat. "Thank you, Miss Fraser." He turned to the crowded schoolroom and nodded. "Thank you."

As he started to step down, Miss Fraser stopped him. "Mr. Hurley, we want you to lead the way to the refreshments, with Mr. and Mrs. Wingate coming next." Miss Fraser's high voice cut into the rising hum of voices and shuffle of feet as people began to move about. "Reverend Appleby, will you ask the blessing, please?"

As soon as the prayer ended, Eliza turned to Vanda. "Shall we find a place in line?"

But at that moment, Cletis tugged on his sister's arm. "Come on, Vanda, Poppa wants to go."

Trennen smiled down at Eliza. "I'd be glad to escort you."

"Miss Jackson." Eliza turned at the sound of James's voice. "You did a fine job tonight."

She smiled at him. "Thank you, Mr. Hurley, but you are the one to be congratulated."

He shrugged. "Spelling was never a problem for me."

"You seem to do a great many things well. My father is very pleased with your work at the cooperage."

"I enjoy my work."

Eliza glanced at her father and saw Mrs. Wingate take him by the arm. She led him to a woman she had been talking to earlier.

"That's good. I think Father enjoys what he does, too."

"Is there something wrong?" James touched Eliza's arm to get her attention.

She lifted concerned eyes to his. "I don't know. Do you have any idea who that woman is my father is talking to?"

He looked across the room. "Do you mean Mrs. Wingate or Mrs. Hurley?"

"Mrs. Hurley?"

He smiled. "My mother."

"Your mother?" Eliza almost choked on the words. She looked again, and recognition dawned in her mind. Of course. That was the woman she had seen with James at church. Mrs. Wingate had said she was a widow. Her father could easily become attracted to such a woman. Eliza knew she attended church regularly, and for her age, she was quite nice looking. Eliza watched her father's smile and easy conversation with the women and felt the noisy, crowded room close in on her.

She turned to Trennen. "I'm sorry, but I don't feel like eating. Maybe some other time. Excuse me."

She grabbed her wrap, fleeing out the door into the cold night. She leaned against the front of the building and looked up at the black, star-filled sky. She thought of her mother and the love her parents had shared. Even after a year, she missed her mother so much. It didn't seem right for Father to look at another woman when he should still be missing Mother as much as she did.

She started as the door opened. "Are you all right?" James asked.

"Of course." Eliza spoke with a sharper voice than she intended and added, "I just needed some fresh air." She brushed past him as she went back inside, leaving James watching her with a puzzled expression.

four

The day before Eliza's birthday she went out back of the house to throw corn to the chickens. They squawked in protest, running a few steps away, only to hurry back and peck a staccato on the ground.

Eliza lifted her eyes to the fields in back of their property and beyond to a distant stand of trees. Autumn colors made a splash across the horizon. She loved fall. It was a time of harvest. A time of gathering in the bounty that God had provided. It was also her birthday.

Father was planning a surprise for her. He hadn't said anything, but she knew. She could hardly wait until tomorrow to discover what it might be.

Eliza ducked her head as she stepped into the dim interior of the small henhouse and gathered a half-dozen eggs. "Good. This is plenty for my cake."

She needed to hurry with dinner because Father wanted her at the chandler shop while he and James made a delivery.

She went in the back door, meeting Lenny in the kitchen.

"Where have you been?" Eliza set her eggs on the table and eyed her brother, dirt-streaked from his head down to his bare feet.

"None of your business."

"That's where you're wrong." Eliza's hands went to her hips. Father allowed Lenny entirely too much freedom, coming and going as he pleased. "As long as I'm the only adult in this house, your whereabouts are my business."

"You ain't no adult," Lenny sneered.

"I'll be nineteen tomorrow, and that's a whole lot more adult than any little ten-year-old boy." She took a threatening step toward him. "How'd you get so dirty?"

He shrugged. "Playin' with the guys."

"What'd you do? Roll around on the ground?"

He grinned. "Part of the time. We were playin' keep away with a wagon wheel rim. It ain't that easy to keep it a-rollin' with three or four guys trying to get it away from you."

"You'd better take a bath before we eat." Eliza pulled the washtub from the back porch. "There's some hot water on the stove. After we add cold, there'll be enough." While she talked, she filled the tub and then dipped her hand in. "This feels fine. I'll give you ten minutes to get that dirt scrubbed off, and then I've got to start cooking. Hurry and get in while I get you some clean clothes."

"Do I have to take a bath?" Lenny whined.

Eliza turned at the door. "Yes. Father wants you to go with him on a delivery this afternoon." Her voice softened at his crestfallen look. "If you stay clean, you won't have to take another bath tonight."

"Another bath?" His voice rose in panic.

Eliza laughed. "You want to be clean for church tomorrow."

When he stared at her, his eyes wide and his mouth open, she pointed toward the tub. "You'd better be in there by the time I come back, or I'll put you in myself. And don't forget your hair."

As usual, Lenny didn't tarry in the water. With his bath out of the way, Eliza had just enough time to mix a cake before she fixed the noon meal. She heard the front door open as she reached for the oven door.

A tendril of hair escaped the confining bun at the base of her head and flew into her eye just as Father came into the room. She brushed at her hair with her left hand while she wrapped her right hand in her apron and reached for the hot pan. Pain seared her finger. The pan clattered to the floor as she jerked her hand back.

"Ow!" She put her finger in her mouth. "Where's the butter?" Tears blinded her eyes.

"Cold water works best." The deep voice and gentle hands guiding her to the sink were not her father's yet were familiar.

She looked into James's gray eyes. What was he doing here?

He pushed her hand into a pan of fresh cold water. She closed her eyes, savoring the relief.

"Keep your hand in for a few minutes." He turned to her father. "Do you have any burn salve and bandages?"

"I think so." It was the first thing Father had said since he came in the door. Eliza could hear him rummaging in the cabinet. She heard someone pick up the cake pan.

"Is my cake all right?" She wiped a hand across her eyes.

"It's fine." James moved back to her side. "How's that hand coming?"

"The water takes the pain away."

He lifted her dripping hand and laid it on a towel. "Let's get your hand dry so we can wrap it."

"Here we go." Father handed James the salve.

Eliza kept her gaze away from James as he blotted her hand. She reached for the can of salve the same time he did. "I can do it."

"Are you sure?" He sounded doubtful.

"Of course. It's just a little burn."

She sighed with relief when the men moved away.

"Is your hand still hurting?" James asked when she joined them at the table.

"Not much." Eliza realized Mother would have been ashamed of her manners. "Thank you for helping me. The cool water took most of the burn out. I'll remember that if it ever happens again."

James smiled. "Let's hope it never does."

As soon as they finished eating, Eliza cleared the dishes from the table and stacked them by the sink. Lenny ran outside, calling over his shoulder that he'd be ready to go anytime.

James shoved his chair back and crossed the room to the sink.

"Do you need help? You don't want to get your hand wet."

Before she could stop him, he was at the stove, bringing the teakettle of hot water. She stepped in front of him to pump cold water into the sink. She pointed to the counter. "Just set it there. I can handle this."

"Are you sure? I don't mind helping." He hesitated. "At

least let me pour the water in for you."

"No. I can do it myself." She knew her voice was sharp, but his presence so close made her jittery. It wasn't right that a man wash dishes.

"Aren't we going to get some of that cake for dessert?" Father asked.

Eliza looked at the cake James had set on the cabinet. She shook her head. "I made it for tomorrow. It isn't even frosted yet."

"That's right. Someone's having a birthday tomorrow, aren't they?"

Eliza turned toward her father in time to see the smiles that passed between the two men. So James knew what Father had planned for her birthday.

"I guess we'll have to wait, James. Eliza's quite a stickler for doing things up right."

Eliza stiffened. Had Father just invited James Hurley to her birthday party?

James went back to the table and pushed in his chair. "I've enjoyed the stimulating conversation and excellent food. Thank you. Maybe sometime you can all come out to my mother's home and share a meal with us."

Eliza heard Father's chair slide under the table. She turned to see him smile at James. "We may take you up on that one of these days."

Eliza frowned as her father and James went into the parlor. Mrs. Wingate should have minded her own business. Father didn't need a wife.

She hung up her apron, looked at the wet bandage on her index finger, and her frown deepened. Maybe she should have let James wash her dishes, after all. Her finger throbbed. She pulled off the sopping wrap and threw it away.

As she tried to wrap a clean strip of cloth around her finger, the kitchen door opened and James stuck his head in. "I thought you might need some help with the dishes. Your father is hitching up the wagon."

"They're all done." She turned her back toward him.

She sensed his presence beside her. "Here, let me do that for you."

"I can do it myself." She was ashamed of the sharp tone in her voice.

"Miss Jackson." He took the cloth from her. "I don't bite. Besides, your father wants to get started on that delivery, and you may as well ride to the shop with us."

Eliza's face burned as she submitted to his gentle ministering. As soon as the bandage was in place, she fled the room, pausing at the door long enough to say, "Thank you, Mr. Hurley."

❧

The chandler shop was quiet with no one next door in the cooperage; so, between customers, Eliza finished her current novel.

While she walked home, she thought of what to fix for supper. Father had said they might not be home until late. Maybe she could fix vegetable soup.

There was no sign of life in the house as Eliza stepped on the porch. She pushed the door open and went in.

"Happy birthday, Eliza." A chorus of voices met her.

Several matches blazed, bringing lanterns and candles to life. Father stood in the middle of the room, his arms outstretched. Eliza moved into his embrace. "Happy birthday, Sweetheart." He gave her a quick hug and kissed the top of her head. "Some of our friends have come to celebrate with you a day early. You don't mind, do you?"

"Mind?" Eliza looked around the room. "Of course I don't mind."

Except for the chairs from the kitchen, there was not a stick of furniture in the parlor. Instead, the walls were lined by people, some she knew and some she didn't. Her eyes met James's briefly. He smiled at her. His sister and mother were there. Miss Fraser. The Wingates. The pastor and his family. Everyone laughed, and the hum of conversation picked up. So this was Father's surprise. She looked at him and smiled. "Someone has been busy this afternoon. Did you really make a delivery?"

He nodded. "Oh, yes. Mrs. Wingate and Vanda spearheaded this renovation."

Vanda hugged her. "Happy birthday, Eliza. This is the first party I've gone to in a long time. We're going to have so much fun. My father couldn't come, but Trennen's here somewhere." She leaned close and whispered. "I think you made an impression on him at the spelling bee."

Others pressed close to speak to Eliza. One by one the older people clasped her hand, saying a few words before moving on through the open door into the kitchen. Eliza could see the table groaning under the weight of the food that had been brought in.

She turned to her father and laughed. "I was worried about getting supper ready, and look at this. There's enough to feed the entire town."

He smiled. "I think that's about how many we'll be feeding. Mrs. Wingate is in charge of serving. I'd better see if she needs anything."

"Oh, Father, shouldn't I help?"

Vanda grabbed her arm. "Not tonight. You're going to stay in here with us and play. We'll eat when the older people are finished."

More than a dozen young people and as many younger children laughed and visited in the parlor. Vanda clapped her hands together and raised her voice. "Mrs. Wingate said we couldn't eat until we've played at least two games." Amid laughter and token protests she continued. "Everyone knows "Skip to My Lou," so grab hands and let's go."

Trennen grabbed Eliza's hand. "I've got my partner." He smiled. "Happy Birthday, Eliza. You sure look pretty tonight."

Eliza returned his smile. "I might have fixed up if I'd known I was going to a party."

His gaze moved over her in a way that brought a flush to her face. "No need. You look perfect to me."

"Thank you." She glanced toward James. He paid no attention to her and Trennen. He was too busy talking to his partner, a girl Eliza hadn't met.

Vanda started singing with the others joining in. "Skip, skip, skip to My Lou, skip, skip, skip to My Lou, skip, skip, skip to My Lou, skip to My Lou, my darling."

Holding Trennen's hand, Eliza skipped around the circle, adding her voice to the others. She cast a side glance at Trennen. With his eyelids lowered lazily, he smiled, and her heart fluttered. After Ralph's rejection she thought she would never look at another man. Now, with Trennen smiling down at her as if she were the only girl present, she wasn't so sure.

❧

Eliza strolled toward town, her surprise birthday party of two nights ago filling her mind. She giggled as she thought of the look on Trennen's face when Joe Martin had grabbed her after "Skip to My Lou" ended. Joe lasted through the next game, then Daniel Ross stepped between them, and so on it went the entire evening. Every game had found her with a different partner. But never James Hurley. He had kept his distance, and she hated to admit, even to herself, that she was disappointed.

Then the adults had come into the parlor to join the fun. When they played "Pig in the Parlor," Eliza noticed that Father picked Mrs. Hurley for his partner.

She and Father had laughed and talked as if they'd known each other for years. Eliza didn't understand how Father could act that way toward a woman other than Mother. He behaved as though he didn't miss Mother at all. Eliza missed her, and seeing Father with another woman stirred the pain of her loss so much more. How she wished Mrs. Wingate had never interfered!

Eliza pushed through the door to Leach's General Store.

"Good morning, Miss Jackson," Mr. Leach's voice boomed from the back of the store. "How are you today?"

"Fine, thank you."

"Thought you might be feeling a bit old after that birthday party." Mr. Leach's broad face beamed at her over a stack of feed sacks.

Mrs. Leach bustled in from the back. "You had a lovely

party." She smiled. "What can I do for you?"

"Father told me to buy some dress fabric as my birthday gift."

Mrs. Leach led her to the bolts of material on a counter against the wall. "That's a wonderful idea. Let's see what we've got." She picked one up, holding it next to Eliza's face. "How about this pretty blue sprig? You've just the right coloring to go with it."

The minutes slipped by while Eliza and the storekeeper's wife selected several pieces of fabric. Finally, they had the yardage cut and folded neatly in a tall stack beside her. Eliza looked at Mrs. Leach with a nervous laugh. "Do you know of a seamstress?"

"I certainly do. The Kowskis are about as reasonable as you'll find, and they're good."

A few minutes later, Eliza left the store with a large bundle in her arms and directions to the Kowskis' house. The package was heavy and cumbersome, so she decided to stop first by the chandler shop to show her father what he had given her.

She found him alone in the back room. She went in and dropped her bundle on the worktable. "What've you got there?" he asked. "It isn't dinnertime, is it?"

Eliza shook her head, smiling. "No, are you hungry?"

He rubbed his middle. "Now that you mention it. . ."

Eliza laughed. "You'll forget all about your stomach once you see what I bought."

Father wiped his hands on his big apron and moved to her side as she untied the paper, letting it fall away. "Well, I'd say you've picked out some pretty dresses. How are you going to get that all sewn up?"

"That's what I wanted to talk to you about." Eliza felt her face flush. "Mrs. Leach gave me directions to some women who do sewing for a living. She says they're very reasonable. But I didn't know if you could afford the extra expense."

Father patted her back. "I'd forgotten which one of you girls was so handy with a needle. It was Cora, wasn't it?"

Eliza nodded. "Cora and Vickie are both good. I couldn't sew a decent seam if my life depended on it."

She heard a noise and turned to see James standing in the doorway.

He nodded to her. "Hello, Miss Jackson."

"Hello." She turned away to cover her fabric, her face burning. She hoped he had not heard her last words.

While James and her father discussed an order for unusual-sized barrels, she prepared to leave. Father hadn't said if she could hire the women to sew for her, but that was all right. She'd ask again later.

She waited until a lull came in their conversation and then spoke. "Father, I've got to get home. I'll see you at noon."

James took a step toward her. "I have a few minutes to spare. I'll walk you home."

Eliza frowned. "That won't be necessary."

"It is if you're planning to take that. You'd never be able to carry it all the way to your house." He took the bundle from her before turning to her father. "This shouldn't take long and then I'll get right on that order."

Eliza turned imploring eyes on her father. "I don't need any help, Father. Maybe he should start the order now."

The twinkle in her father's eye was unmistakable. "James knows what he's doing. Getting you home is more important than any order."

Eliza stretched to her full height. "Father, I've never needed assistance finding my way before."

"But you've never had such a big package to carry." He grinned, obviously enjoying her discomfort.

Eliza turned, defeated, toward the door. Her father's words followed her. "Go ahead and hire those ladies to sew your dresses for you."

Eliza went through the shop into the autumn sunshine without a backward glance. She turned toward home, walking in a near run.

ja.

James followed Eliza, watching her ramrod-straight back with an amused grin. It was obvious she didn't want his company—just as obvious as it had been the night of her party.

He'd been unable to get near her for all the other fellows.

Her package was heavy, but mostly it was cumbersome. Strong as he was, he felt the pull on his arms before they had gone far. Of course, it might be easier handled if he didn't have to go in a half run to keep up with her. He tried to think what he might have said to offend her but could think of nothing.

He shifted the package to his shoulder, taking the strain off his arms. How was she going to get it to the dressmakers'? He took a few running steps to overtake her as she started down the Booneville Road.

"Would you mind slowing down?"

"You may stop and rest if you're tired." Her cute little nose went into the air.

"Miss Jackson, I'd like to ask you something, and it's all I can do to keep up."

Her pace slowed.

She acted like his little sister in a snit. He tried again. "Once I get started on that barrel order, I won't have much time. Have you considered how you're going to get your dress goods to the dressmakers'? Right now, I've got the time to deliver it. Wouldn't it make sense to take it there instead of your home?"

As fast as she'd been walking, James wasn't prepared for her sudden stop. He also wasn't prepared for the flashing brown eyes she turned on him. "So you did hear."

He hesitated, uncertain what was wrong. "Hear what? When we left your father said—"

"That since I can't sew, I'll have to go to the dressmakers'."

Her large brown eyes glistened. He nodded—then shook his head—confused. "No, that wasn't exactly what he said."

She shrugged, straightening her shoulders again. "He might just as well, because it's true. But I don't think you should go with me."

"Why not?"

Her eyes met his. "Because I don't want you to."

"Oh, really?" He grinned, intrigued by her show of independence. "I'll tell you what I'll do. I'll carry your fabric to the dressmakers' house, and then I'll leave. Is that a deal?"

Her eyes never left his. "Do I have a choice?"

"No." His grin grew even wider, and he was sure he saw an answering one tug at the corners of her mouth before she twirled away.

This time, as she turned back, she slowed her gait. James walked behind and to her side. He didn't want to overstep the boundaries she had put between them until he was sure where he stood with her. Somehow, Eliza Jackson had caught his fancy. As he watched the proud set of her shoulders, he determined to find a way to break down the wall she had erected against him.

❧

When they reached the dressmakers' home, Eliza took the package from James and thanked him. His cheerful whistle as he tripped down the steps toward town brought a smile to her lips. She knocked on the door of the small cabin, hoping Mrs. Leach's directions had been correct and this was the right place.

A girl near Eliza's age opened the door. A smile of recognition crossed her face. "Eliza Jackson, how nice to see you again."

Eliza looked from the friendly green eyes to a sprinkling of freckles covering the girl's alabaster skin. Her deep auburn hair was long and curly, pulled back at the nape of her neck to hang free down her back. Eliza remembered seeing her at church and at her party, but she couldn't remember her name.

"Miss Kowski?" At least Mrs. Leach had told her that much.

"Oh, please, call me Kathrene." She stretched out a small, dainty hand and grasped Eliza's arm. "Come inside. I want you to meet my mother. She didn't go to your party. She had some work to finish and wouldn't take the time."

Eliza followed Kathrene into a cheerful sunlit parlor.

"Mother, this is Eliza Jackson. I went to her birthday party Saturday night, although I don't think she remembers me." An impish grin lit Kathrene's face as she looked at Eliza.

Eliza couldn't help blushing any more than she could stop the laughter that escaped at her own expense. "I'm sorry. It's just that there were so many there." She smiled at the woman sitting in a chair in front of the window. "I'm pleased to meet you, Mrs. Kowski. I'm in need of a seamstress, and Mrs. Leach recommended you."

Mrs. Kowski pushed the garment she was working on to the side and stood, stretching her back as she did. "How nice of Mrs. Leach. Here, set that package on the couch. It must be quite heavy."

Kathrene and her mother could have passed for sisters. *Almost twin sisters,* Eliza thought as she looked from one to the other.

"It is a little heavy." Eliza deposited it on the couch and untied the string.

"I love to look at new fabric." Kathrene pulled the paper back and lifted the first piece. "This is so pretty. You'll be beautiful in it."

Mrs. Kowski thrust a magazine into Eliza's hands. "This is the latest *Lady's Book.* See if you like anything."

"Won't you need a pattern?" Eliza wasn't sure, but she thought Cora had always used a muslin pattern for their dresses.

Kathrene laughed. "Don't worry, Mother will make a pattern from the sketches in the magazine."

"Oh." Eliza was impressed with a talent she knew little about. She perched on the edge of a chair and thumbed through the magazine until she found a dress that she thought would be perfect for church.

"Could you make this one from the blue print?" She held the page for Mrs. Kowski to see.

"Yes, I think the blue print is a good choice for it. Would you like to pick out the rest or wait and see how this one turns out?"

Eliza stood. "I'd like to look further, but it's time now for me to be home fixing my father's dinner. If you made your own dresses, I'm sure mine will turn out fine."

Mrs. Kowski smiled as she set the magazine aside. "Before you leave, may I take a couple of measurements so I can cut out your dress tonight?"

A few minutes later with the measurements recorded by Eliza's name and a price agreed upon, Kathrene walked out to the front gate with her. "I really enjoyed your party Saturday night."

Eliza smiled. "I'm glad you came. I'm sorry I forgot your name. We've been here just a month now, and I've met so many people I have trouble remembering everyone."

A warm smile lit Kathrene's face. "I'll just have to make myself more noticeable from now on."

"I thought you would be two older women, maybe sisters. Then when you turned out to be my age, I was a little nervous about letting you know I couldn't sew. I thought you might laugh at me." Eliza smiled.

Kathrene shook her head. "I could never laugh at someone else when there are so many things I can't do." She laughed softly. "My mother is a wonderful cook, but I think she's about despaired of ever teaching me."

Eliza took Kathrene's hand and squeezed gently. "Speaking of cooking, I've got to go. I'm really glad I got to meet you."

Kathrene nodded. "Let's make ourselves known at church, too. I've seen you each week, and now I'm ashamed I didn't introduce myself."

Eliza edged toward the road. "That's all right. I didn't do any better Saturday night." She waved as she started down the dirt road toward home. "Come over and visit me sometime."

"All right, I will." Kathrene stood by the gate to wave before turning back inside.

Eliza thought Kathrene was every bit as nice as her best friend, Grace Newkirk, from back home. Now she had two new friends, Vanda and Kathrene.

She hummed "Home, Sweet, Home" until she caught sight of her father's shop. Only to herself would she admit that James had been right. She would have struggled to carry her package as far as he did. She appreciated his help but wished she wasn't so attracted to him.

five

"Oh, Eliza. It looks perfect on you." Kathrene clasped her hands under her chin and sighed. "You have such beautiful coloring."

After several fittings throughout the first part of November, Mary and Kathrene had finished the first dress.

Eliza smiled. "Thank you."

Mary Kowski bustled in from the other room. "Here are some more magazines you may look at for the rest of your dresses, Eliza."

Eliza smiled at Kathrene's mother. "Thank you. I love this one."

She still found it hard to believe that Mary Kowski was old enough to be Kathrene's mother. Mary's energy seemed boundless as she rushed from one project to another.

Several minutes later, Eliza hurried home with a light step. With Mary's and Kathrene's help, she had picked out the other three dresses.

That night just before bedtime Father said, "I've been doing some thinking about Christmas."

"Christmas is more than a month away, Father." Eliza looked from her father to her brother. Lenny just shrugged his shoulders.

Father smiled. "Yes, I know. But it may take us that long to get ready. I'm just getting started on the bayberry candles. Your dresses are not finished. We should be looking for gifts. And we mustn't forget, it's a two-day trip even in good weather."

Lenny's eyes grew wide as Eliza leaned forward. "What are you talking about, Father? A two-day trip where?"

"Oh, did I forget to mention that?" The twinkle in his eyes

warned Eliza that Father had something special planned.

"Yes, you did."

Lenny looked smug. "I already know."

"How could you? Father, did you tell—"

"No." Father shook his head. "I didn't tell Lenny anything."

"All right, Smarty." Eliza turned to her brother. "Where are we going for Christmas?" The words had no sooner left her lips than she knew. She jumped from the chair and flung her arms around her father's neck. "Home. We're going home to see everyone for Christmas, aren't we?"

"Where else would we go that takes two days?" Lenny's look of scorn was lost on Eliza's enthusiasm.

"How can you do that? What about the shops?" Eliza asked.

Father made room for Eliza on the couch. "James can handle anything that comes, and if not, he can close up until we get back."

"Yeah, it'll probably snow, and we won't go, anyway." Lenny hid his eagerness behind a look of indifference.

"You've got a reasonable concern there, Son." Father's smile disappeared for a moment. "But the weather has been unusually mild so far, and according to the almanac, it should be for awhile."

"Oh, Father, you're right. There's so much to do." Eliza began counting on her fingers. "I'll have to prepare food for the trip. I want to bake something special to take. We need to take gifts for everyone. What do you think they'd like?" Before he could answer, she smiled. "We'll see Nora and Christopher, too. I just know they've grown."

She swung toward her father as a new thought entered her mind. "Are we bringing Nora home?"

Father shook his head. "I want that more than you know, Eliza. But I don't see how we can at this time. The shops are just getting started, and I need your help much too often for you to tend an active two year old, too. But soon we will."

They talked, making plans until it grew late and Father sent them off to bed.

෨

Their coming trip dominated the conversation at breakfast the next morning. Father swallowed his last bite of biscuit and pushed his chair back. "I've been thinking we ought to invite our old friends for Christmas dinner."

Lenny looked up. "I'll bet the Newkirks will come because Ben's married to Esther. But what about the Starks? Aaron will come with Cora, so that just leaves Ralph and Ivy."

At the mention of Ralph's name, Eliza's spoon dropped to the table. She hadn't thought of him. In all the excitement of seeing her family again, she had forgotten Ralph. But of course he would be there. With his wife and baby. She gathered the dishes from the table while dread crept over her soul.

"It looks like your sister's ready for us to get out of her way, Lenny." Father stood and stretched. "I'll lay aside the next batch of bayberry candles to take back for the girls. I'll be working on them today. How'd you like to come down and tend the shop this afternoon, Eliza?"

"Fine." She pulled Lenny's spoon from his hand as he shoveled in the last of the oatmeal. He swiveled around with a frown. "Hey, can't you wait until a guy finishes?"

"Good, then I'll see you later." Father guided Lenny toward the door. "Tell your sister bye and thank you for breakfast."

Lenny turned to peek under his father's arm at Eliza. He crossed his eyes and stuck out his tongue. "Good-bye, Eliza, and thank you for what I got to eat before you jerked it away."

Father's back was turned as he pushed through the kitchen door into the parlor. Eliza lifted a heavy iron skillet as if to throw it at Lenny. "I'm glad you enjoyed it, little brother. Would you like some of this, too?"

Lenny ducked under his father's arm and ran through the door. By the time Father looked at Eliza she was drying the skillet. She smiled at him. "Bye, Father. I'll see you at noon."

When the front door closed behind them, the house grew quiet, allowing memories of Ralph to beat without mercy against Eliza's heart. How could she go see the man she'd thought she would marry when he was married to another? She finished the dishes and hung the wet tea towel on a rack to dry. She put beans on the stove to simmer, yet the image of Ralph would not leave. She moved to the bedrooms, making beds, straightening, dusting, and sweeping. Still Ralph haunted her.

With sudden determination, she ran to the kitchen, shoved the beans to the back of the stove, and grabbed a heavy, woolen shawl. There was plenty of time to see Kathrene and Mary Kowski before noon.

The fresh air felt good on her face as her feet carried her to the small cabin across town. Kathrene opened the door at her knock.

"Eliza, come in." Kathrene's smile of welcome gave a sparkle to her green eyes.

"I didn't intend to come today, but I have wonderful news, and I need some adjustments made." Eliza moved into the room past Kathrene.

"What is your news?" Mary gave Eliza a warm hug.

All thoughts of Ralph faded as Eliza sat on the couch between the two women and told of her eagerness to see her family at Christmas. "I'd like my other three dresses adjusted to fit my sisters."

"Oh, Eliza, how sweet of you." Mary patted Eliza's hand.

Eliza smiled at her friend. "I want the pink for Esther. It's soft and feminine just like she is."

Mary smiled and stood. "I'll get some paper and a pen to write down the changes we'll need to make. Are the girls much different in size from you?"

Eliza frowned as she brought each to mind. "No, not really. Esther's taller and a little thinner. Cora and I always wore each other's clothes, so there shouldn't be any changes to make there. Vickie is older, but she's probably an inch shorter than Cora and me. She has two children that she says have made her fat, but she really isn't."

Mary wrote, trying to keep up with Eliza's descriptions. "Then you think Vickie might be just two or three inches larger around than you?"

Eliza nodded. "Yes, that's about right."

"All right." Mary laid the pen and paper down. "I think I have enough here. Why don't you pick out the fabric you want for each sister?"

"I think Esther should have the pink, Cora the blue, and Vickie the green calico."

As she left, she touched Kathrene's arm. "Please pray for me while I'm gone."

"Of course. Mother and I both will. Besides safe travel, is there something special we should be praying about?"

With a sigh, Eliza met her friend's concerned gaze. "There was a young man." She hesitated as moisture threatened her sight. "He married someone else." She took a deep breath and brushed a hand across her eyes. "Just pray that if I see them, I won't make a fool of myself."

Kathrene gathered her into a hug. "I understand. I'll pray that God will show you He has something better for you than what you lost."

Eliza straightened and smiled. "Thank you. Now I've got to run home before Father gets there. I may have burned beans for him to eat if I don't hurry."

Kathrene laughed, calling after Eliza's retreating figure, "I burn them when I'm right there watching. Yours will be fine."

True to Kathrene's prediction, the beans had cooked down but were not scorched. Lenny and Father each had two bowls full.

At the shop that afternoon, Eliza kept busy most of the time. A customer left just as Vanda came in.

"I didn't expect to see you." Vanda smiled.

"Does that mean you wouldn't have come in if you'd known I was here?"

Vanda laughed. "Of course not. It means I'd have been here sooner so we could visit longer."

"You say all the right things, but that doesn't explain why I've scarcely seen you all this month." Eliza pretended to pout.

Vanda picked up a bayberry candle from the counter and sniffed it. "My father hasn't been working as much so I've had to stay close to home." Her smile didn't reach her eyes. "He has some old-fashioned ideas about women. He doesn't like for me to be away from home any more than necessary." She quickly changed the subject. "M-m-m. These really smell good, don't they? What are they?"

Eliza glanced toward the candle in Vanda's hand. "Bayberry. Father's making them for Christmas. I've sold several today."

A wistful sound came into Vanda's voice as she put it back. "Maybe nearer Christmas I can get one. But for now we just need the cheapest candle you have."

Eliza came around the counter. "You know, we do have a candle that costs a little more, but in the long run it's more economical because it lasts so much longer."

"Oh, really?"

Encouraged by Vanda's interest, Eliza reached for the special candles and handed one to her friend. "These are made with whale blubber and burn as long as three or four tallow candles. The light is brighter, too. But they only cost about twice as much."

"H-m-m. That sounds like a good deal." Vanda smiled. "I'll take two of them."

The bell above the door rang as Eliza wrapped the candles for Vanda. She looked up, meeting James's gaze.

"Good afternoon, ladies." His presence seemed to dwarf the room.

Eliza returned to her work, her hands trembling as she tied the string. Vanda smiled at him. "Good afternoon, yourself." She turned back and tapped Eliza's arm. "I believe he was speaking to both of us."

Eliza lifted her gaze to the gray eyes watching her. A half grin sat on his lips. She felt a stirring deep inside that she didn't want to feel. "Hello, Mr. Hurley."

His lips spread into a full smile.

She felt her face flush. Why did he have to look at her like that? "Is there something you need? My father is in the back room."

He shivered violently. "B-r-r-r. We may get that first snow before Christmas, after all." He grinned, doffed an imaginary hat, and strode across the shop. He stopped, turned, and nodded with a big grin at Vanda before disappearing through the back door.

As soon as the door closed, Vanda turned to Eliza. "Why did you treat him so cold? It's obvious he likes you."

"Likes me!" Eliza's voice rose. "Where'd you get an idea like that? He was rude to me."

Vanda laughed. "He wasn't rude. He was just reacting to the way you patronized him. Just because he's your father's employee—"

"Oh, Vanda," Eliza interrupted. "I didn't mean it that way. It's just that he makes me nervous. Here are your candles. I think you'll like them very much. They are about the only kind I use at home."

Vanda reached for the bundle, a smile softening her face. "James Hurley likes you, and I think he has caught your fancy, too."

Eliza didn't answer except to tell Vanda good-bye as she left. While her friend was right about Eliza's feelings for James, Eliza couldn't allow herself to like him. Ralph's rejection still hurt too much for her to trust her heart to another.

The shop filled with customers, so she was busy when James walked back through on his way to the cooperage.

six

Eliza could scarcely sit still when Cedar Creek and then the log cabin came into view. A wave of homesickness for her mother swept over her. She watched the closed door of the cabin coming closer, half expecting Mother to be standing there, waiting with a welcoming embrace. But Esther opened the door.

Esther laughed as she stepped out to greet them. "Father. Eliza and Lenny. Oh, Ben will be so surprised."

Father gave her a warm hug. "Where is my oldest son?"

"At the barn. We have a cow down that he's taking care of." Esther looked as beautiful as ever. Her wheat blond hair, done up in a loose bun, fell in a soft wave across her forehead. Her lips, full and pink, curved up at the corners.

Father looked toward the building that had served as shelter when they first moved to the country. "Lenny, you can help me with the horses. We'll see what Ben's up to."

Eliza stepped through the heavy oak door ahead of Esther, allowing memories of the three happy years she had spent there to course through her mind.

"I'm so glad you came." Esther hugged Eliza. "Your sisters and Ben will be thrilled. We all talked the other night about how hard it would be to have a real Christmas with you gone. Why don't we invite everyone over to share Christmas Day with us? Grace will want to see you."

"That would be wonderful." Even as Eliza agreed, a twinge of fear struck the pit of her stomach. "Everyone" included Ralph.

"You must be worn out from your trip and probably hungry, too." Esther turned toward the kitchen. "Did you get any sleep?" Esther stirred the fire in Mother's old cookstove while Eliza stifled a yawn.

She laughed. "Some. I didn't feel tired until you started talking about it. Even now, I'm so excited I don't think I could rest."

Esther smiled. "That's good, because I expect Ben will have your sisters here before we finish eating."

"Is there anything I can help you with?"

Esther shook her head. "No, you go greet your brother."

Ben crossed the room in long strides and grabbed Eliza in a warm hug.

Father and Lenny followed him into the room. Ben turned to face them, his arm still around Eliza's shoulders. "I'm having trouble believing you're here. We'll have a real Christmas, after all."

"Yes, if gifts are not important." Esther's soft voice brought a groan from Ben.

"Oh, I forgot. We didn't know you were coming."

"Don't worry about gifts." Father laughed. "Eliza already said the best gift she could get is coming home for Christmas."

Eliza nodded as everyone looked at her. "That's true. I just want to be with my family. What could be better than that?"

Ben smiled. "Of course you're right." His eyes, so like their father's, twinkled. "The only problem is, I saw your wagon. It's loaded to the top."

"Yes, and we need to unload." Father jammed his hat back on his head. "Come on, Ben. Show us where you want these supplies. We need to lighten the wagon for our return trip. Then someone needs to tell Cora and Vickie we're here."

As soon as Cora and Aaron arrived, Eliza ran from the cabin with her father and Lenny behind her while Ben and Esther waited on the porch.

Aaron lifted Cora from the horse's back, holding her waist until he was sure she had her footing. Cora smiled up at him. "I'm fine, Aaron, really."

Eliza pushed past her brother-in-law to catch her sister in a fierce hug. She laughed. "Are you surprised to see us?"

"Yes and very glad."

Then Lenny and their father pulled Cora away, and Eliza stepped back. It was good to be home.

"How you been doin', Eliza?"

She looked up into Aaron's bright blue eyes. How much like his brother Ralph he looked! She ignored the pounding of her heart and smiled at her brother-in-law. "Just fine. I'm so glad we could come home."

"Yeah. Ben said we'd have a big Christmas dinner. Be jist like old times, won't it?"

Her heart lurched at the thought, but she managed a weak smile. "Yes, it should be really nice." She thought of Aaron and Ralph's sister. "How's Ivy getting along?"

Aaron smiled. "She's doin' real good. That little fellow of hers ain't no bigger'n a minute, but he sure runs her a merry chase. He's already crawlin'."

Eliza laughed. She tried to imagine Aaron's sister as a mother. It was hard to see anything but the sullen girl she had been before her marriage to Mr. Reid. "Is Ivy happy?"

Aaron grinned. "Happy as a pig in the wallow."

"I'm glad she's happy. It'll be good to see her."

"You're the one I want to visit with." Cora linked her arm in Eliza's as they turned toward the house. "We've got three months of catching up to do. You're going to tell me all about that big city you live in and what you've been doing there."

"Don't worry, I will."

"Here comes Nicholas." Lenny's excited voice drew attention to the trail behind the house. Although Lenny was several years older than his nephew, the two boys had always been close.

Eliza and Cora followed the others to meet their sister Vickie and her husband John. But it was their oldest son, Nicholas, who scrambled from the wagon before it stopped and ran past them to grab Lenny.

"Let me have those babies." Father reached for Christopher and then waited while John set Nora on his other arm and then turned to help Vickie.

After a warm hug from Vickie and John, while the others visited, Eliza watched the two little ones look at Father with solemn faces. She noticed his eyes were moist as he clutched them close. Nora lifted a tiny hand to her father's cheek. "You mine papa?"

A smile lit his face. "Yes, I am."

"Me, too." Little Christopher reached up to tug on his chin.

Father smiled down at his grandson and kissed his cheek. "I'm Grandpa to you."

"Eth. Bampa." Christopher nodded his head while Nora snuggled against her father's chest.

"Well, it looks like they haven't forgotten Father," Eliza said.

"Of course not, and they haven't forgotten you, either," Vickie spoke beside her. "It seems like a lifetime, but you've only been gone a short while."

Cora pulled Eliza by the hand. "Let's see if we can get Nora away from Father."

Nora stared at Eliza with wide brown eyes. Slowly a shy smile tugged at her mouth, and she leaned forward.

It wasn't hard to talk Vickie into letting Nora spend the night. Eliza took advantage of the short time with her little sister before John came midmorning the next day to take her back home so she wouldn't be in the way of Christmas preparations. Ben and Father made the rounds of the neighbors, inviting them to Christmas dinner, while Esther and Eliza cleaned house and baked a wide assortment of pies and cakes.

That afternoon, Cora and Aaron came. They hadn't been there long before Cora took Eliza's hand and pulled her toward the door. "Grab your wrap. We haven't had that talk you promised me." She nodded toward the ladder leading to the loft. "We can't share our secrets up there anymore. Now we have to go outside where we can find some privacy."

"Don't you girls be gone long. When Vickie and John get here, we'll open gifts." Their father's eyes twinkled. "You won't want to miss that."

Cora laughed. "You're right, we won't. We'll come right in when they get here."

"So tell me what it's like in Springfield," Cora said before they stepped off the porch.

Eliza described the house and shops. She told about the church and several of the people she had met. "I've made two friends. Kathrene Kowski helps her mother as a seamstress. They are both wonderful. I know you'd love them, too."

She went on telling about the friendship that had grown between herself and Kathrene. Then she said, "I have another friend, Vanda Von Hall. Vanda reminds me of a will-o'-the-wisp. I don't know where she lives, and she doesn't come to church often. I only see her when she comes to me."

Cora shook her head. "She sounds strange."

"Oh, but she isn't. Actually, she's very nice." Eliza defended her friend. "I've met her father and brothers. They seem nice, too."

"Brothers?" Cora smiled. "And how old are they?"

"One is Lenny's age."

"And the other?"

"About twenty-one." Eliza's face felt hot in the cold air.

"So have you met any other young men, or is this the one?" Cora grinned at her sister's discomfort.

Eliza turned to face Cora. "I don't have to settle for the first man who looks my way. Father gave me a surprise birthday party, and I'll have you know I was the most sought after girl there." She interrupted as Cora started to speak. "No, I wasn't the only girl."

Cora laughed. "I'm glad to see living in the city hasn't changed you."

Eliza relaxed as she laughed with her sister. "I don't know if I've changed, but I do know it's good to be home for awhile."

"Only awhile? Does that mean you're anxious to get back?"

Eliza thought of the well-furnished, roomy house awaiting them and shrugged. "I suppose in a way I am. It's nice having my own house to care for, even though sometimes I'd like to turn all the work over to someone else."

Cora didn't speak for several moments and then said, "Have you considered that Father might marry again?"

Eliza's heart lurched as she thought of Mrs. Hurley. She turned on her sister. "How can you even think such a thing? He loved Mother too much to desecrate her memory."

"But Father is still young enough to have. . ." She paused, then added, "Feelings."

Eliza stopped near a young apple tree, its bare branches moving in the cool air. "If you don't mind, I'd rather find out about all of you. And don't tell me Vickie is going to have another baby. I already know."

Cora laughed. "You always know." She paused. "Almost everything."

"Do you mean Esther?"

"How did you know she was, too?"

Eliza shrugged. "By the way she acts, and I thought I noticed a difference in the way she looks."

Cora shook her head. "You are a wonder, but you don't know everything."

Eliza looked at her sister. What had she missed? Then she noticed the protective way Cora's hand rested on her abdomen. With a glad cry she threw her arms around her. "You, too? Oh, Cora, that's wonderful. No wonder you look so happy. I thought it was because you're so much in love with Aaron."

Cora laughed. "Well, of course, I am." She patted the slight bulge under her coat. "But I already love this little fellow, too."

The jingling of harness and rumbling of a wagon announced John and Vickie's arrival. Eliza looked toward the west as they came into view and began to laugh.

"What's so funny?" Cora touched her arm. "We promised Father we'd come right in when Vickie got here."

"But that's just it." Eliza could scarcely get her breath. "We have to open gifts now." She wiped her eyes, trying to stop laughing. "I just realized I had dresses made for each of you, and not one of you will be able to fit in them."

Cora linked her arm through Eliza's. "If you think you're going to take the dresses back, you can think again. We'll just save them until we can wear them." She smiled. "Come on, let's beat Vickie and John to the house."

Eliza enjoyed the time spent with her family as they gathered around the Christmas tree and exchanged gifts. Both Father's bayberry candles and her dresses were welcomed. She sat on the floor with Nora snuggled in her lap. She couldn't resist squeezing her little sister, knowing that their time together was short.

⸎

Eliza woke the next morning to a churning stomach that could be attributed to only one thing. Before the day ended, she would see Ralph.

Esther's father and mother came early with their seven children and more than enough food for everyone. Eliza grabbed her friend Grace in a welcoming hug. "It seems like ages since I saw you last."

Grace squeezed Eliza. "What do you mean, 'seems like'? It has been ages." She pulled away and looked at her friend. "This is the lonesomest place ever with you gone. What's it like where you live? You've got to tell me all about it."

The girls wandered off arm in arm, falling into the easy friendship they had known before. Eliza spent the morning close to Grace, watching and listening for Ralph. Each step on the porch or opening of the door caused her heart to quicken, but he still had not come by midmorning.

"Is that a wagon I hear?" Vickie pulled the kitchen curtains back.

Cora looked over her shoulder. "It's Ivy and Mr. Reid." She turned to Eliza. "They have the sweetest little boy."

Eliza saw Ivy, still seated in the wagon, hand down a blanket-clad bundle to her husband. "I can't see him. Ivy looks well, though."

"I think you'll appreciate the change in her, too." Cora laid a hand on Eliza's shoulder. "Becoming a mother made her a different person. Of course, the real change came when Ivy accepted Jesus last month."

"Oh, that's wonderful!" Eliza smiled as Ben opened the door.

Ivy's long, shiny black hair was done in a braided coil on top of her head. Her carriage rivaled that of a queen as she stepped into the house with a warm smile. "Ben, it's good to see you."

Ben nodded to Ivy and shook hands with her husband. "Good to see both of you, too. All three of you." He lifted the baby's tiny hand in his large one. "This little fellow gets bigger every time I see him."

Cora stepped forward to greet her sister-in-law with a quick hug. "Ivy, I'm so glad you came. Now Eliza can see you while she's here and get to meet my nephew."

Eliza started to shake hands with Ivy but was surprised when she received a hug instead. "You've given us all a nice Christmas gift by coming home for a visit."

"Thank you, Ivy." Eliza didn't know what to make of the changes she could already see. Ivy had always been beautiful, but now a look of radiance surrounded her.

As the Reid family mingled with the others, Eliza stole a quick glance through the window across the field to the woods.

"I think we're ready to set the table." Vickie's voice put Eliza back to work.

Several minutes later, Eliza stood at the end of the table with Grace and counted the place settings. "Will there be enough room for everyone? We squeezed in ten places here at the table. What about the others?"

"Howdy, folks." Ralph's cheerful voice rang out, sending a chill down Eliza's back. "Reckon you'uns thought we wasn't gonna make it."

"No, we knew long as there was food awaitin' you'd git here, Ralph," Aaron greeted his brother.

Eliza stood, her hands gripping the back of the chair in front of her.

"Eliza." Vickie's hand felt gentle on her shoulder. "We can eat in shifts or spread out into the other end. It's warm enough so the older children can eat outdoors."

Eliza nodded. Her senses numb, she heard the hum of conversation mingling with childish shouts. Yet through it all, Ralph's voice sent waves of warmth to her face. She turned slowly, hoping her cheeks were not as red as they felt.

He stood, as handsome as ever, talking with the other men. She almost hated him for being so good-looking. Then his eyes lifted to hers, holding her gaze for a heartbeat. She turned away. She was glad when the men moved outside.

"Do you mean you walked with the baby? I figured you'd hitch that old ox up to something." Ivy took the baby from Anna.

"Ralph broke the axle on that wagon you gave him, and he's never gotten around to fixing it." Anna shrugged. "It wasn't so bad, though. Ralph carried the baby part of the way."

"Oh!" Ivy's foot hit the floor. "Sometimes I have trouble believin' Ralph's my brother." Her voice softened as she turned back to Anna. "Mr. Reid and I will take you and the baby home."

"Thank you, Ivy." Anna's pale blue eyes looked tired. "I'm sorry we didn't bring anything. Ralph said not to. He said it'd be too hard to carry."

"He was right." Cora smiled at her sister-in-law.

Eliza kept her distance from both Ralph and Anna. In the crowded house it wasn't hard, yet their presence seemed more real to her than those with whom she visited.

The men and children came inside, and then Father prayed. The children took heaping plates to the porch, while the women relaxed in the parlor end of the large room to feed the babies, and the men sat at the table.

Eliza vied for the privilege of helping Nora. She soon found there was little she could do as Nora insisted on feeding herself.

But Ralph didn't appear to have the independence of a two year old. As Anna fed mashed potatoes to their nine-month-old son, Eliza heard him call his wife.

"Hey, Woman!" His voice carried over the steady hum of voices. "Get me some coffee."

Anna set the baby on the floor and made her way to the kitchen.

Aaron looked across the table at his brother. "Why don't you get it yourself? Ain't you got legs?"

Ralph grinned. "Sure do." He nodded toward his wife. "See 'em comin'?"

Aaron's dark brows drew together. "One of these days, Ralph, somebody's gonna set you down."

Ralph grinned and took the coffee Anna handed him.

Anna had her baby cuddled in her arms, nursing him, when Ralph called again. "I'm needin' some of that pie, Woman."

Ivy jumped up, handing her baby to Cora. She looked at Anna. "Doesn't he even know your name?"

Anna sighed. "It's just his way."

Ivy snorted. "You sit still. I'll take care of my lazy brother."

Eliza watched Ivy stalk to the sideboard at the far end of the kitchen. She picked up a pie and headed for Ralph. She lifted a piece of blackberry pie and slapped it upside down on Ralph's plate, juice splattering everywhere.

Her softly spoken words barely reached the women. "I know you're too lazy to scratch your own itch, Ralph, but if you bother Anna again, you'll be eatin' the rest of your food off your lap."

Ralph looked up at his sister in surprise. "What got your back up? Cain't a man eat in peace?"

"Just be sure that's what you do. And let Anna have some peace, too." Ivy rejoined the women, took her baby from Cora, and sat back down.

Anna gave her a wan smile. "Thank you, Ivy."

"I don't know why you put up with him." Ivy shook her head. "If Mr. Reid did me that way, I'd be hurt plumb through."

Anna shrugged. "I don't mind."

The women had to clean the table before they could eat and then clean again when they finished. Esther peered into the water bucket. "We're out of water for the dishes. I guess I'd better ask one of the men to get some."

"I'll go," Eliza said. A trip to the well by herself would be a welcome relief.

She picked up the empty bucket and, threading her way through men and smaller children, went outdoors. The cool air against her face felt good. She could see Lenny and Nicholas playing with the Newkirk children. Their childish laughter filled the air. She envied them their innocence.

Eliza lowered the water bucket into the well until she heard it splash and sink. She tugged on the rope to pull it up. When Ralph's voice startled her, she dropped the rope, turning to find herself less than a foot from him.

At the sound of the bucket hitting the water again, Eliza swung back and grabbed the rope.

"I said howdy, Eliza."

She fought to control the pounding of her heart.

"Ain't ya gonna say nothin'?" Ralph persisted.

Eliza set the full bucket on the rim of the well and faced him. "Hello, Ralph. It's nice to see you again."

A familiar grin spread across his face. "It's right nice seein' you, too."

Ralph was handsome, and he knew it. She stood under his spell, unable to control her heart.

"Come walk with me a ways. I'm full as a tick." He reached out.

She started to take his hand; then, as if a fog lifted, she saw him as she'd never seen him before. He needed a shave and a haircut. A bath wouldn't hurt. He had a wife, yet he asked another woman to walk with him. He was lazy and inconsiderate, with no respect for his wife.

The image of James Hurley filled her mind. He worked hard at his job. He was always clean about his person and in his speech. James was a Christian. Ralph was not. How could she have spent so much time yearning for a man who could never be faithful to anyone, not even his own wife?

She shook her head. "I don't think so, Ralph."

"Come on, Eliza. It'll be like old times." He grinned his

most persuasive. "I missed you."

A sudden flash of anger struck her. "In case you hadn't realized, you're the one who up and got married."

"Now, Eliza, you know that weren't my idea."

She gave him a withering look. "I feel sorry for Anna. I wouldn't go across the yard with you, Ralph. Go back inside and get your wife if you want someone to walk with."

She pivoted away from him toward the well, shutting him once and for all out of her life. Freedom such as she hadn't experienced for almost a year released her heart.

She picked up the full bucket of water, turned around, and shoved it at him, splashing the front of his shirt. "Here, take this to the house so we can wash dishes. It'll make a good impression on your neighbors—and your wife."

Not waiting for him to talk his way out of it, Eliza went to the house. Happier than she'd been in a long time, she announced, "Ralph's bringing the water."

Ralph followed her with the bucket balanced in his right hand, a frown on his face.

Ivy laughed. "I don't know how you did that, Eliza, but you'd better tell Anna your secret."

Eliza smiled. "Oh, Anna, Ralph told me he wanted to go on a walk. Why don't you go? There's enough of us to do these dishes and watch your baby for you, too."

Anna's tired eyes shone as they met her husband's. He looked from Eliza to Anna, and a good-natured grin lit his face. "Guess I know when I'm whipped."

Anna took his hand. "Since I don't have to walk home, I'd be proud to go with you, Ralph."

seven

Winter remained mild with little snow. In the months following their brief visit, Eliza missed her family even more. Each day she longed for the time when Nora could come to Springfield where she belonged. Yet she had much to be thankful for. No longer did Ralph's image haunt her. How could she have thought she loved such a lazy, faithless oaf?

"Spring's just around the corner."

Eliza turned from the dishes at her father's voice.

"It doesn't look much like it." She glanced toward the window where the bare oak branches stood out cold and forlorn. "Of course, no more snow than we've gotten, it hasn't felt like winter, either."

"That's true." He grinned. "I ran into Miss Fraser downtown." He pulled out a chair and sat down. "Miss Fraser has decided the perfect way to raise money for the school would be a box social."

"When will it be?"

"She wasn't sure. The first month without an *r* in it, I think she said." He grinned at Eliza. "I've been thinking. You'll need a new dress to wear. Why don't you pick something nice out and take it to your seamstresses?"

"That sounds like a good idea." Eliza laughed with her father.

❧

The box social was set for the first day of May. Eliza woke early to prepare a tempting meal. A young fryer from the chicken coop went into her skillet, and potatoes boiled in a pan on the stove. She decided to make two blackberry tarts for dessert. Once they were in the oven, the potato salad could be made.

She tied the handles of her wicker basket together with a

bright red hair ribbon, then stood back to admire her work. She nodded with satisfaction as her father came into the kitchen.

"Are you ready to go? I've got the buggy hitched."

Eliza smiled. "Oh, so we're going in style today."

"Of course." Father reached for her basket. "We don't want anything to happen to this." He lifted it, pretending to almost drop it. "What have you got in here? It weighs a ton."

"Oh, Father." Eliza laughed. "I know it isn't that heavy. It's just potato salad, chicken, and tarts."

"Can we go now?" Lenny ran into the kitchen, slamming the door behind him. "I'm starving."

"Which reminds me." Father set Eliza's basket back on the table. "Did you fix enough for Lenny?"

"Of course." Eliza stepped to the cook table and picked up another box. "This is for you and Lenny. It's a good thing you said something, because I almost forgot it."

Father took the box in one arm and carried the basket in the other. As he went out the door, he grinned down at his son. "Looks like you'll have plenty, Lenny. I'll be eating some other lady's cooking today."

Eliza's heart sank as she followed him to the buggy. She thought he had lost interest in Mrs. Hurley. By the time he parked among the other wagons and buggies, she decided that if there were any way possible to keep him away from Mrs. Hurley, she would do it.

Eliza's feet slowed as she neared the table set under a tree in the middle of the yard. Mrs. Hurley stood behind the table holding a white box with a sprig of goldenrod tied on the top. Eliza watched her place it on the table and walk away.

Eliza walked around the table. She set her basket in front of Mrs. Hurley's box. Then in one quick motion, she pushed the box to the center of the table between two others. To make sure it was one of the last auctioned off, she covered it with her own basket.

"Are you guarding the food, or did you just get here?" A

voice at her elbow startled Eliza.

"Oh, Kathrene. And Mary. I didn't see you come up." Eliza smiled at her friends. She held out her skirt in a curtsy. "How do you like my new dress?"

Mary straightened the collar in a motherly gesture. "I do believe you look prettiest in blue."

"Thank you." Eliza watched as her friends added their colorful boxes to the growing pile on the table. "Everyone will want to eat with you. Your boxes are so pretty and clever."

"Well, they aren't so pretty underneath. That's why we covered them with fabric scraps." Kathrene adjusted the ribbon on hers. "Of course, the food is delicious since Mother wouldn't let me help."

"I believe they're about to begin." Mary touched Kathrene's arm. "Let's move to the shade of that tree."

Eliza saw her father nearby talking to James and his mother. Her emotions churned as she watched. Then her eyes shifted to Mary. Maybe she could talk Father into buying Mary's dinner. A smile sat on Eliza's lips. It might work.

After the minister prayed, the auction began. One after another, the boxes sold, and the couples separated from the others to share the contents.

Eliza saw James and Mrs. Hurley walk away from her father. Seizing the opportunity, she stepped to his side.

Father grinned at her. "See that big box on the end? I'll bet it's got a good meal inside."

Eliza had no idea to whom it belonged, and she didn't want to take the chance. She shook her head. "No, just because it's big doesn't mean anything. Look at those two on the other side."

"In brown paper?"

"No, in calico. One is Kathrene's, and the other is her mother's. I know they'll be good."

"Your seamstresses?" The tone of his voice made it sound as if a woman couldn't do two things well.

"I'll have you know Mrs. Kowski is a good cook," Eliza announced.

"In that case, I'd better buy her box." Father was joking, but Eliza grasped his words as a lifeline.

She smiled. "Oh, yes. You will, won't you? I know you won't regret it." The auctioneer picked up the one next to it and began his chant.

A frown touched Father's forehead. "Which lady is Mrs. Kowski?"

"She's standing over there by that tree with Kathrene."

He looked where she indicated, and his eyes widened. "Do you mean the two little redheaded women? I've seen them at church and thought they were sisters. Which one's the mother?"

Eliza laughed. "Mrs. Kowski is on the right."

Father turned back without a word as the auctioneer picked up one of the fabric-covered boxes. Eliza nudged him. "That's it, Father. That's Mrs. Kowski's."

"Now what am I bid for this pretty box. Why, if the food inside's half as good as the covering, it oughta be worth a dollar. How about it? Do we hear a dollar?"

Father raised his hand. "I'll bid fifty cents."

"I got fifty cents. Do I hear seventy-five?"

Eliza held her breath. If Father didn't get Mary's box, there would be nothing she could do to stop him from buying Mrs. Hurley's.

After bidding it up to one dollar and a quarter, the auctioneer stopped. "Sold to the gentleman who keeps us in light." Father claimed his meal amid laughter.

"I believe I just bought your box, Ma'am." He offered his arm to Mary.

Eliza was surprised to see a faint blush touch Mary's cheeks. She smiled up at him and slipped her hand under his arm. "Perhaps we should find a place to eat, then."

Kathrene giggled as they walked away without a backward glance. "Well, well, imagine my mother walking out with a man after all these years."

Eliza stared after the departing couple. Her victory left a bitter taste. "What do you mean, walking out? This isn't a social engagement. We're here to raise money for the school."

Kathrene's eyebrows raised. She turned back, clasping her hands. "Look, my box is next."

"Yes, and there's Charles Wingate waiting with a smug expression on his face." Eliza inclined her head toward the young, well-dressed gentleman. "We know who you'll be eating with, don't we?"

Kathrene just smiled.

"Well, looky here. If there isn't another pretty one." The auctioneer held up Kathrene's box. "Let's see if we can start this one at a dollar. How about it?"

Charles's hand shot up. "I'll bid a dollar."

"Make it one-fifty." A stranger spoke from the edge of the crowd.

"One-fifty it is. Do I hear two?"

Charles nodded.

"Two and a quarter." The stranger's dark eyes flashed a challenge.

"Two-fifty." Charles ignored the auctioneer.

Kathrene's face flushed as she watched the two men battle over her box. Eliza nudged her. "Who is he?"

Kathrene shrugged. "I've never seen him before."

"Well, he wants your box awfully bad." Eliza stared openly at the tall young man. His dark brown hair blew across his forehead in a gust of wind. Eliza could see that he was quite handsome.

Charles called out, "Five dollars."

The stranger bowed toward his opponent. "Enjoy your meal."

Charles smiled and nodded. He held out his hand to Kathrene. "Let's find a quiet place to eat."

Eliza watched Kathrene glance over her shoulder toward the stranger. He caught her gaze and smiled.

After a couple more boxes sold, the auctioneer picked up Eliza's basket. "A finer-looking container than this couldn't be found today, gentlemen. I hear tell the contents are just as fine. What'll you give for a chance at this good meal?"

"A dollar." Again the voice of the stranger called out.

Eliza's heart quickened. Would her basket go as high as Kathrene's? She glanced toward James. Would he counterbid?

He stood in a group of men, his arms crossed. His eyes met hers. He grinned and shook his head. Her face flamed. The nerve of him. She hadn't asked him to bid on her basket. She turned her back to him.

"I was told you are the young lady I'm to eat with." A deep voice by her side spoke.

Eliza looked into the stranger's deep brown eyes. She'd been so busy fuming about James that she hadn't realized her basket sold. Without thinking, she asked, "How much did you pay?"

His eyes twinkled as his lips lifted in a lopsided grin. "Exactly one-fifth of my present assets."

At her blank look, he took her arm to lead her away. "This day finds me a poor man, Miss . . . ?"

"Jackson." Her heart quickened at his masculine good looks. "Eliza Jackson."

"Miss Jackson. I paid one dollar for your basket and from the weight. . ." He lifted it toward his nose and sniffed. "And the aroma, I'd say I got a bargain."

Her face grew warm as her lashes lowered. "You flatter me, Mr. . . " She looked up at him. "I don't know your name."

"Stephen Doran, Miss Jackson."

❧

Kathrene lowered her coffee cup and smiled at Eliza. "The box social yesterday was a success, wasn't it?"

Eliza stared across the kitchen table at her friend. "A success?"

Disaster would be a better word. James hadn't bid on her basket. Stephen Doran's bid was the only one she got, and then when they joined Kathrene and Charles, he scarcely noticed her. She couldn't even bring herself to think of her father and Mary.

Eliza tried to not listen as Kathrene chatted about how much her mother had enjoyed Father's company.

One thing was certain. Mary had kept Father away from

Mrs. Hurley. The entire afternoon, Eliza had seen him only once when he'd told her he was giving her friend a ride home and would come back for her and Lenny.

"Don't you think so, Eliza?" Kathrene's voice cut into her angry musings.

"Think what?"

"Stephen Doran. Don't you think he is quite handsome?" Kathrene's green eyes sparkled.

Eliza stood and walked to the sink. "You know he only bought my box so he could get close to you."

"Why, Eliza!" Kathrene's eyes widened. "Have you taken a fancy to Mr. Doran?"

Eliza let out a short laugh. "How could I take a fancy to someone who spoke no more than two sentences to me? I notice he found plenty to say to you, though." She crossed her arms. "Didn't you feel sorry for Charles? I'm sure he felt as left out as I did."

"Left out!" Kathrene jumped up, setting her coffee cup on the table with a loud *thunk*. "I think you're jealous."

"Jealous?" Past hurts and frustrations boiled in Eliza, spilling over into words she didn't mean. "How could I be jealous of you? I have everything I want right here." Her hand swept out. "You can have your Stephen, and Charles, and James, and every other man in town if you want them. I certainly don't."

"And you think I do?" Kathrene's eyes flashed. Her freckles stood out against her white face. "If that's what you think of me, I won't trouble you with my presence."

Kathrene wrenched the kitchen door open and stomped through the parlor. The bang of the front door echoed through Eliza's head, accusing her.

A verse from the Bible came to her mind. "For jealousy is the rage of a man: therefore he will not spare in the day of vengeance." Tears welled in her eyes. Kathrene was right. She was jealous.

Before she could move, the door opened and Kathrene peeked around the edge. "I'm sorry, Eliza. May I come back in?"

Eliza nodded, meeting her embrace.

"I shouldn't let my temper get away from me," Kathrene said.

"No, I started the whole thing because my pride was hurt by a stranger we'll probably never see again." Eliza wiped her eyes.

"Let's agree that no man will ever come between us," Kathrene said.

Eliza nodded.

≈

"We've been invited to dinner at the Kowskis' Sunday after church," Father announced that evening. His wide grin gave him a boyish look.

Sunday at the Kowskis' was all Eliza had feared it would be. Her father and Mary kept up a lively conversation about church happenings, discussing the sermon that morning and their hopes for the young man who came forward for prayer.

Lenny remained quiet throughout the meal except when he asked for more to eat. Eliza frowned at him, but he didn't notice. When he finished his second helping, she picked up her own and Lenny's plates. "I'll wash the dishes, and then we need to be getting back home, don't you think, Father?"

He groaned and patted his stomach. "I don't know if I can move. You've outdone yourself on this meal, Ma'am." He smiled at Mary. "It was even better than the box social."

"Thank you." She gave him a warm smile. "I enjoy cooking."

Eliza stood and moved to the wash table. Mary's hand on her arm stopped her. "Leave the dishes to Kathrene and me. You're our guest."

Kathrene laughed. "Yes, Eliza. I may not be able to cook, but I can wash dishes."

Eliza smiled before turning to her father. "Don't you think we should be going? I'd like to rest before church tonight." She stepped toward the door.

Father pushed his chair back and stood. "Come on, Lenny. You heard your sister." He looked at Eliza with an affectionate smile. "I don't know what I'd do without my little girl. She's taken over the running of the house and Lenny and me." He patted her shoulder. "Does a real good job, too."

She looked up at him with accusing eyes. "Thank you, Father, but Mother was a good teacher."

Mary met her stony gaze with a warm smile. "Your mother must have been a wonderful woman to have raised such a beautiful daughter."

Eliza's lashes lowered. "Thank you, Mary. Yes, my mother was a wonderful woman."

But was she the only one who thought so? Father seemed to have forgotten his late wife as his interest in Mary grew. At church that evening Father sat beside Mary.

eight

Eliza watched her father's relationship with Mary develop and knew she could only blame herself. One day, toward the middle of June, he came into the chandler shop and told her Mary had agreed to become his wife.

After he left, Eliza stood in the middle of the floor while the words *He doesn't mean it* kept running through her mind.

"Did I catch you daydreaming?" James's voice penetrated her befuddled brain.

"What do you want?" Did he always have to catch her at a disadvantage?

"I have a question for your father."

"He isn't here." Eliza didn't want to be rude to James, but she couldn't seem to stop.

"It's a good thing you don't have any customers." James lounged against the counter.

Eliza turned her full gaze on him for the first time since he came into the shop. "Why?"

A slow grin spread his mouth. His eyes twinkled merrily. "Because, Miss Jackson, an old grouch like you would drive a less brave person away. What's got your back up today?"

Her hands clenched at her sides. "My father."

Sandy-colored eyebrows arched above his gray eyes. "Your father?"

"He says he's getting married."

"To Mrs. Kowski?"

She nodded. Tears filled her eyes. "Oh, James. . ." Her voice broke, and she found herself leaning against his chest. His arms encircled her as the tears fell.

After awhile she stepped back and blew her nose. "I'm sorry. I don't usually cry in public."

"No one's here but me." James smiled tenderly at her. "Are you going to be all right now?"

She tried a smile of her own. "I don't think I'll ever be all right with my father remarrying. But I'm okay now. Thank you."

"I guess I'd better get back to work then." James moved to the door. "When your father comes back, would you tell him I need to ask him something?"

She nodded.

He opened the door. "And, Eliza. . ."

She looked at him.

"If there's anything I can do, you know where to find me."

When her father returned, Eliza told him James had been looking for him. He went to the cooperage and stayed there the rest of the day.

A couple of days later Eliza came into the house from the garden with her apron full of new potatoes and green onions. Father and Lenny sat at the kitchen table.

"You mean I get to stand up in front of the church with you?"

"That's right." Father smiled at his son. "I think you're old enough to do that, don't you?"

Eliza tried to ignore them as she set the vegetables out on her work counter. Lenny didn't understand what it would do to their lives if Father remarried. Eliza picked up a potato, washed it in a pan of water, and began scrubbing the soft skin off.

"What about Eliza?" Lenny asked. "She gonna do somethin', too?"

"Of course." Eliza could feel her father looking at her, but she refused to turn around. "Mary wants Eliza and Kathrene to stand beside her to demonstrate that we'll all be one family." Father cleared his throat. "Why don't you run along so I can talk to Eliza now?"

"Okay." Lenny slammed the door on his way out.

Eliza stiffened when her father moved to her side.

"I'd like for you to be happy for us, Eliza." Father's voice was low and pleading.

A flush moved over Eliza's body. So Father knew how she

felt. She sighed. She never had been good at keeping her feelings to herself. "I don't want you to marry her, Father. How can you replace Mother so easily?"

Her father flinched as if she had hit him. "I loved your mother. I still love her memory and always will. Mary is not a replacement for Mother. I will never forget your mother, Eliza. But I love Mary for herself, and I intend to marry her for that reason."

"I don't want you to marry her, Father," Eliza repeated with stubborn determination.

When her declaration met with silence, she turned toward him. The saddest look Eliza had ever seen covered his face. "I love you very much, Eliza, and I'm sorry you feel this way; but in all honesty, I have a perfect right to remarry. I'm trusting God that in time you'll accept it. In the meantime, Mary is waiting for you to pick out your dress."

Shame for her thoughts and words filled her heart. Still, she could not bring herself to accept her father's decision to remarry. "I don't need a new dress."

Father frowned. "Go to Leach's this afternoon and get some fabric to take to Mary. She's got enough to do without waiting until the last minute to make your dress."

Eliza knew she had pushed her father far enough. She nodded and turned back to her vegetables.

Eliza walked to town that afternoon, kicking at every rock in her path. She crossed the square and entered Leach's General Store.

"Good afternoon, Miss Jackson," Mr. Leach greeted her. "What can I do for you?"

"I'd like to look around, if you don't mind."

"Not at all. Make yourself at home." He turned back toward the door as the bell rang again.

Eliza wove her way through the barrels and counters of merchandise toward the stacks of fabric along the far wall. She held a blue silk up to her face.

"That's very beautiful," Mrs. Wingate spoke beside her.

Eliza lifted her head in surprise. She hadn't heard anyone approach. "Yes, it is."

"I understand your father and Mary Kowski will be married in a few weeks."

Eliza shrugged. "Yes, I suppose so."

Mrs. Wingate laid a sympathetic hand on Eliza's arm. "Don't you think your father ever gets lonely?"

"He has Lenny and me. Why would he need anyone else?"

"You won't always live at home." Mrs. Wingate smiled. "Eliza, many older people who have lost their spouses remarry for companionship and to share the burden of living."

Eliza remembered her father's confession that he had eaten downtown before she and Lenny came. He loved Mary's cooking. Surely, Father's marriage would be one of convenience. When Mrs. Wingate left, Eliza turned back to the fabric with a lighter heart.

Mary finished Eliza's dress the day before the wedding. When she went to pick it up, Kathrene met her at the door. "Mother went to town with your father, but I guess you already knew that."

"No." Eliza frowned, hurt that Kathrene knew her father's whereabouts when she didn't.

Kathrene pulled her inside. "Come and see what I've got." She pointed at a small round table by the window. An assortment of wildflowers filled the vase sitting in the center.

"Where did you get those?"

Kathrene blushed. "Do you remember Mr. Doran, the young man who bought your box at the social?"

How could she forget?

"He gave them to me." Her voice dropped to a whisper. "He asked me to walk out with him."

"You didn't. . . ?"

Kathrene shook her head. "No, of course not. We know nothing about him."

"What about Charles?"

Kathrene flashed a smile. "What of Charles? He's a good friend, nothing more."

Eliza followed her into the bedroom, where her dress lay across the bed. She couldn't help noticing the sparse furnishings in the small cabin. Kathrene and her mother shared the double bed that took up most of the floor space in the small room. Her bedroom was twice the size of theirs.

Eliza scarcely noticed her dress as she looked around the small cabin. Her eyes rested on the cracked chinking in the walls, and she wondered how the women survived the cold winter winds. Mary had good reason to marry her father.

She smoothed the billowing blue silk skirt and smiled at Kathrene. "It's very lovely, as is all your work. I'll wear it proudly when I stand beside you tomorrow."

❧

"Dearly beloved, we are gathered together. . ."

It was a lie—the five of them standing up together as one family. Eliza tried to forget where she was. She did fine until the minister turned to her father.

"Wilt thou love her, comfort her, honor, and keep her, in sickness and in health; and, forsaking all others, keep thee only unto her, so long as ye both shall live?"

A hard, empty ball expanded inside her stomach. Surely she had never missed her mother more than at that moment.

As in a dream, Eliza watched her father slip a gold wedding band on Mary's finger. The minister said, "I now pronounce you man and wife. What, therefore, God hath joined together, let not man put asunder."

Eliza bowed her head with the others as the minister prayed, but she did not anticipate his words when the prayer ended.

The minister nodded to her father. "You may kiss your bride now."

Father gathered Mary into his arms. Eliza stared hard at the floor. How could he kiss her? Mercifully, the moment was over quickly.

Kathrene elbowed her. "We're supposed to follow the bride and groom outside."

"How wonderful! You two girls are sisters now." Mrs. Wingate stopped them near the back door. "Congratulations."

"Thank you, Mrs. Wingate," Kathrene answered for them both.

Charles stepped around his mother as she turned away. He smiled at Kathrene. "May I have the pleasure of your company for dinner?"

"We would be honored, wouldn't we, Eliza?"

"You go. I'll eat alone." Eliza dropped Kathrene's arm and slipped outside into the fresh air. She had never felt so alone in her life.

She crossed her arms, leaning her shoulder against a tree. A slight breeze ruffled her hair. She lifted her face to it, closed her eyes, and let it cool her cheeks.

"Eliza," James's low voice intruded.

Again he appeared at the worst possible time. She opened her eyes to look at him. "What do you want?"

He laughed. "Your use of the English language never ceases to amaze me. Are you always so stingy with words, or is it just with me?"

She sighed. "I'm sorry. It isn't you."

He grinned. "Good. I wanted to ask you to eat with me." His voice lowered. "I know you're having a hard time today. I'd like to help if I can."

Eliza gave a short laugh. "I don't think that's possible. They're already married."

"Sometimes having a friend helps."

"A friend?" Eliza hadn't thought of James as a friend before
• and wasn't sure she wanted to. She suddenly realized that "friend" didn't sound like enough.

At his nod, she smiled. "All right."

She looked up, saw Vanda approaching, and called to her. "I was afraid you wouldn't be here."

Vanda's laugh brightened Eliza's mood. "Me? Miss my best

friend's father's wedding? Not on your life."

She looked at James.

Eliza moved away from the tree. "James is eating with us. Is that all right with you?"

Vanda shrugged. "Sure, but I think we'd better be going if we're going to get anything."

They reached the grounds set aside for the dinner just as the minister prayed. Mary and Father led the line and then sat at a special table prepared especially for them. A white cotton tablecloth covered the rough wood, giving the table an elegant look.

Vanda peered closely at her friend. "Do you think you'll like having a new mother?"

Eliza's eyes narrowed. "You mean stepmother, don't you?"

Vanda nodded. "I guess that answers my question."

"I don't mean to be so snappish. This whole thing has been a strain."

"Maybe we should get in line." James touched Eliza's arm.

Lenny and Cletis ran past. "Hey, you gonna stand there and let all the food get ate up? Come on. We'll let you get in front of us."

Vanda lifted her eyebrows. "I wonder why they're so interested in us all of a sudden."

They wound around tablecloths spread on the ground picnic style and people with their plates piled high. Lenny and Cletis stepped back for each of the stragglers until the last guest was in line.

Vanda frowned. "They must be up to something."

James laughed. "They're boys. Boys are almost always up to something."

"I suppose you know from experience?" Eliza realized she felt better. James was right; she had needed to be with friends.

"Of course." He grinned down at her, making her heart do flip-flops.

Eliza smiled but agreed with Vanda. She knew her brother.

Sometimes Lenny was more than she could handle, and as much as she liked Vanda, she realized his behavior had gotten worse under Cletis's influence.

As Eliza filled her plate, she saw Lenny and Cletis scramble from under the table where Mary and Father sat. The boys ran a short distance away. They stood behind a large oak tree, their hands stifling giggles, their eyes dancing in merriment.

She kept them in sight as she ate. She was certain they had pulled a prank on Father and Mary, but she couldn't think what it might be. With her attention divided, she kept up her end of a lively conversation with James and Vanda.

Vanda glanced over the crowd. "What happened to our brothers? I forgot to watch them."

Eliza nodded toward the oak tree. "They're standing over there." Even as she spoke, the merriment went out of the boys' faces. Lenny's eyes grew wide. Cletis grabbed his arm, pulling him back.

"What on earth are they doing?" Vanda sounded as puzzled as Eliza felt.

"Maybe we'd better find out what they've already done." Eliza looked toward the table where her father sat. Father and Mary were visiting with others who had joined them. Eliza let her gaze roam over the table, trying to find something out of place.

And then she saw it. A thin wisp of smoke curled upward from the end of the table. As she watched, the smoke disappeared in a sudden burst of flames.

"Fire!" Eliza's outcry created pandemonium. Father lifted Mary from her seat. With one arm around her, he tossed his glass of water on the flame. Others followed his lead as they scrambled back from the burning cloth.

"Cletis and Lenny did that, didn't they?" Vanda searched through the excited crowd. "Where are they?"

Eliza pointed. "They just ducked behind that tree."

The two girls set off in a run to catch their brothers. As angry as Eliza was at Lenny, she was even more angry with herself. She had known he was up to something, and she hadn't stopped him.

Vanda grabbed Cletis first and held tight in spite of his squirming attempts to escape. Lenny ran a few steps before Eliza caught his arm. He turned wide, fearful eyes on her. "We didn't mean to, honest."

"That's right. We didn't make any fire." Cletis tried to wrench out of Vanda's grasp. "Ow! You're hurtin' me."

"I'll hurt you a whole lot more if you don't tell the truth." As Vanda reached for a better grip on her brother, he jerked free. He stumbled from the sudden release, then took off running. Vanda turned a troubled face toward Eliza. "I hate to think what Poppa will do to him when he finds out. I'd better catch him." She left in a run, calling over her shoulder, "I'm sorry."

Eliza watched her for a moment before turning toward the crowd gathered around the table. She looked down at Lenny. "Well, are you going to tell me what happened, or would you rather tell Father?"

He shrugged his shoulders. "I told you we didn't mean to."

Eliza closed her eyes for a moment, then looked at her brother. "Lenny, you obviously did something, even if you didn't mean to. What did you do?"

He clamped his lips shut, looking defiantly up at her.

"All right, then." Anger welled up in Eliza as she pulled him toward their father.

nine

Lenny trembled beneath Eliza's hands. Her anger turned toward Cletis. How dare he run off and leave Lenny to take the blame for what he had instigated!

"Leonard Jackson, do you know what this is?" Father held a small object between his fingers.

Lenny nodded. "It looks like an old firecracker, Sir."

"It's a firecracker, all right, but it's not old, and you know it." Father pointed a finger at Lenny. "Go to the buggy and wait until we come."

Lenny jerked from Eliza's grasp and ran. Eliza looked up, meeting the gray eyes of James Hurley. "I hope your father isn't too hard on Lenny."

"Why? Don't you think he deserves to be punished?"

He shrugged. "Probably, but I doubt there's a man here that hasn't pulled a stupid trick like that at some time in their lives. It's part of growing up."

"Trying to blow up the table your father is sitting at is more than a stupid trick."

James laughed. "That little firecracker wouldn't have done much more than make a big noise."

"But it didn't make any noise. Instead it made a fire." She crossed her arms. "You know, what's bad is that Cletis Von Hall got away, and he was probably the one who did it. Lenny was just with him."

James lifted his eyebrows. "In that case we'd better hope that Vanda doesn't tell her father what happened."

"Well, I should hope she would," Eliza said. "He deserves to be punished even more than Lenny."

"I suppose, but—"

"Eliza, are you ready to go?" Her father stood with his arm

around Mary's waist. "Kathrene is coming later with Charles."

Eliza looked at James. "I guess I need to go."

He nodded. "I'll see you at church tonight." He turned and walked away.

&.

As soon as they entered the house, Father laid a gentle hand on Eliza's shoulder. "Would you mind going upstairs? I need to talk to your brother alone."

Eliza sat on the stairs out of sight while her father decided Lenny's punishment. When Mary suggested he not play with Cletis for two weeks, she crept upstairs to her room.

Eliza felt the strain of the day especially at supper that evening. As soon as her father laid his spoon down, she pushed her chair back, picking up her bowl. "I'll wash dishes."

"No, Eliza," Father said. "The dishes can wait. Mary and I have something to say."

Father looked first at Eliza, then Lenny, and finally Kathrene, before his eyes met Mary's. She nodded slightly.

He smiled at her and began. "Mary and I have decided it would be good for us to go away for a short time."

"Where are we goin'?" Lenny asked.

"Not all of us, Son." Father ran his hand over his thinning hair in a nervous gesture. "I meant just Mary and me."

Lenny frowned. "What do you wanna do that for?"

Kathrene leaned forward, a smile on her face. "I think that's a wonderful idea. When will you be leaving?"

"In the morning." Father turned to her. "I just need to speak to James tonight, we'll pack a few things, and then try to get as early a start as we can tomorrow."

"Well, don't worry about us. We'll get along just fine." Kathrene shared a smile with her mother.

Eliza shrugged when her father's gaze met hers. "Sure, we'll be fine."

Father's hazel eyes darkened. He reached across the corner of the table to clasp her hand. His voice was soft. "Eliza, we're going after Nora."

Eliza sat in stunned silence until she pulled away from her father, her chair crashing to the floor as she sprang up and ran from the room, the dishes forgotten.

Emotions she didn't understand flooded her being as she stumbled up the stairs to her room. For almost a year she had planned to go with Father when he brought her sister home. Now Mary would be the one. Mary would take over her sister, her father, and even her house. She fell across the bed to release a torrent of tears into her pillow.

❧

Sometime later, a tap on the door brought Eliza upright. "Who is it?" Her voice sounded hoarse from crying.

"Kathrene. May I come in?"

Eliza scrambled from the bed and across the room to her washbasin. She splashed cool water on her face and blotted it with a towel. She moved to the door, smoothing her wrinkled dress with her hands.

If the remains of her crying bout were still on her face, Kathrene made no notice. She stepped into the room, a gentle smile the only evidence of her concern. "They sent me to tell you it's time to get ready for church."

"You're glad, aren't you?" Eliza struggled with the hooks on her dress.

"Glad about what?" Kathrene's hands felt cool against her back as she helped.

Eliza stood still to let Kathrene unfasten her dress. "All of it. Your mother. My father."

"In a way I am. Mother has been alone so long. I'm happy she has someone to love and to love her."

Eliza felt tears burn her eyes. "What about your father? Have you forgotten him? I haven't forgotten Mother and neither has my father. He'll never forget her. He'll always love her."

"Oh, Eliza, of course I haven't forgotten my father."

Eliza turned and saw the matching tears in Kathrene's eyes. "Mother will always love him. But I should hope there's room in her heart to love your father, too."

&

The evening service passed in a blur until James stopped her after church. Concern softened his expression. "Are you all right, Eliza?"

"Do you know how many times you've asked me that in the time you've known me?"

He smiled. "No, it does appear to be a habit I'm developing."

"I don't know if I'll ever be all right again. When my mother died, my world was turned upside down. It just seems to get worse every day."

"I'd like to help if I. . ." His voice trailed off as Eliza's father placed a hand on his shoulder.

"Mr. Hurley, you are just the person I need to talk to."

Eliza backed away. She felt betrayed and cheated as her father made arrangements to return to their wilderness home without her.

When they got home, Mary turned toward Father's bedroom, her bonnet and their Bibles clutched in her arms. Eliza stared at her as she went through the door.

"Come on, Eliza." Kathrene tugged on her arm. "There's no towel in my room. Where do you keep them? Your father said he didn't know."

Eliza followed Kathrene up the stairs.

Kathrene led her to the guest room and stepped inside. Eliza pulled the middle drawer of the chest of drawers open to reveal neat stacks of towels and washcloths. She looked at the bed where Kathrene's dress of the afternoon sprawled where it had been thrown. A petticoat lay in a circled heap on the floor as if she had just stepped out of it. Even Cora hadn't been this careless with her things.

Kathrene pulled a washcloth and towel from the drawer and turned to the washbasin, a bright smile on her face. "This room is so wonderful. I've never had a room all my own before. And this is such a big, pretty room. I love it."

Somehow the idea that Mary had married Father for their house eased Eliza's pain.

Eliza pushed her bedroom curtain aside and looked out. In the early morning light she watched her father's wagon move slowly out of the yard. A movement on the seat in front caught her eye. Father waved at her. Mary, sitting beside him, looked up and waved, too.

Eliza hadn't found it in her heart to see them off like Kathrene and Lenny had. As soon as breakfast was over, she had told them good-bye and retreated to her room. She lifted her hand for a moment and then let the curtain drop back into place.

She sank to her bed, where she stayed until a knock on her door interrupted her time of self-pity. "Eliza, please, may I come in?"

"What do you want?"

There was a moment's silence, and then Kathrene said, "It's Lenny. I can't find him."

"He's probably outside playing."

"I don't think so. He was in the house reading while I washed the breakfast dishes. I went out to feed the chickens, and when I came in, he was gone."

"Those chickens are mine. Father bought them for me." Eliza pulled the door open to glare at Kathrene.

"I know they're yours, Eliza. I was just feeding them." Kathrene's voice was soft. "I thought you might want some time alone this morning."

Eliza's gaze dropped to the floor, her conscience pricked.

"I've looked everywhere, Eliza. I don't know what else to do. Your father said Lenny was not to go anywhere without our permission. Don't you think we should do something?"

Eliza shrugged and met Kathrene's worried gaze. "He's probably run off to play with Cletis. He'll come home as soon as he gets hungry."

A spark of green fire lit Kathrene's eyes. "He's disobeying his father, and I'm not going to let him get away with it. We have a responsibility to see that Lenny obeys. If we don't stop him now, he won't listen to a thing we say the entire two weeks our parents are gone."

Finally Eliza nodded. "All right. Let me get my bonnet. I'll go downtown and see what I can find out." She turned back into the room.

"Shouldn't I go, too?" Kathrene followed her. "Isn't there someplace I could look?"

Eliza tied her bonnet under her chin. "No. I think you should stay here in case he comes back."

"I suppose you're right." Kathrene looked doubtful. "But if he isn't back by dinner, I'll go with you this afternoon."

Eliza laughed off Kathrene's concern. "Oh, don't worry, he'll be here when it's time to eat."

The midmorning sun warmed her back as she tried to imagine where little boys went on summer mornings. She knew they sometimes rolled wagon rims across the square. Maybe James had seen Lenny.

Eliza went to her father's shops. James was busy with a customer, so she stepped inside and waited.

After placing his order, the man left, nodding to Eliza. James looked up with a smile. "I didn't expect the pleasure of your company today. What can I do for you?"

"I'm looking for Lenny and thought you might have seen him."

James's smile disappeared. He shook his head. "No, I haven't seen him. Is something wrong?"

She shrugged. "Probably not. He just left home without permission."

"I'll close up shop and help you look."

"No, that's not necessary." She stepped back. "I'm sure he'll come home at noon to eat."

James shrugged. "All right. I'll keep an eye out. Maybe he'll come by."

"Thank you." She turned and ran from the shop. She asked Mr. Leach and looked everywhere she could think but didn't find him.

Kathrene and Eliza ate a hurried meal at noon. Eliza expected any moment to hear the front door open and see Lenny come in demanding food. But he didn't.

"Where should we go?" Kathrene placed her plate on the counter. She turned as Eliza started to speak. "And don't tell me I have to stay home again. I won't do it. I may be just a stepsister, but I care."

"All right, we'll go together." Eliza sighed. What if Lenny wasn't with Cletis? What if something terrible had happened? She didn't know where to look for him. Surely she had exhausted every possible place that morning.

"Where will we look?" Kathrene asked again.

"I guess we could go back to town." She stood and picked up her plate. "Maybe Mr. Leach has seen him since I was there."

But Mr. Leach shook his head. "No, I haven't seen him since church last night."

"Where do we go now?" Kathrene asked.

Eliza looked across the square at the cooperage. Should she check back with James? She knew he would willingly drop whatever he was doing to help them search. While she tried to decide, she saw Vanda walking toward them.

"There's Vanda. Maybe she knows something."

The girls met in the middle of the square.

"Have you seen Lenny?"

"Have you seen Cletis?" Both spoke at once.

"That settles it." Eliza sighed. "They're together, but where are they?"

"I don't know." Vanda frowned. "Cletis slipped out early this morning after my father left. I managed to keep his stupid prank yesterday quiet, but if he doesn't get back home before long, there'll be nothing I can do."

"Have you talked to Trennen? Maybe he has seen them." Eliza felt as if she were grasping for straws.

Vanda nodded. "I just came from the Wingates'. Where have you looked?"

Eliza's hand swept out in an all-inclusive gesture. "Everywhere we could think of. Do you know of any special places they might go?"

Vanda looked thoughtful. "Have you looked at the creek?"

"I didn't know there was a creek." Eliza's eyes grew wide. Until that moment she hadn't thought that Lenny might be hurt. "You don't think they've drowned, do you?"

"No, I didn't mean that." Vanda started across the square. "There's a creek just northwest of town. It has a quiet spot where the boys like to swim. As warm as it is today, they might be there."

The girls turned down the dirt road leading west out of town. Eliza sighed, and Kathrene looked at her. "It is terribly warm, isn't it?"

She nodded. "I understand if they went swimming in this heat, but Lenny's still in trouble."

"Cletis, too. It isn't much farther." Vanda pointed to their right. "Just beyond those trees."

Before they were through the trees, Eliza heard laughter. Her temper flared, and she ran into the clearing on the bank of the creek. Lenny was there, all right. So were three other boys, including Cletis. And all were stripped to the bare skin.

"Oh, my." Kathrene's soft gasp as she came up behind Eliza stopped the boys' horseplay, and all four dove under the water.

Cletis was the first to break the surface with a ferocious scowl. "Get outta here. Go on. Beat it." He hit the water toward them.

The other boys came up for air one at a time. Guilt sat on Lenny's face even as he frowned at Eliza. "Yeah. Go away." He copied his friend.

Eliza wasn't sure what to do. The boys' clothing was scattered along the bank where they had let it fall. She knew they couldn't come out of the water as long as the girls were there, yet how could they be trusted to come if someone didn't stay and enforce it?

Vanda planted her hands on her hips. "Cletis, if you don't

get out of there, I'll come in and get you." She picked up some pants from a pile of clothing, then stepped to the edge of the creek, her feet just inches from the water. "Here, put these on."

"I can't. I'll get 'em all wet. What do we gotta get out of here for, anyhow?" Cletis asked. "We ain't hurtin' no one."

"Poppa's going to be home in a couple of hours, Cletis. You know that."

The change in Cletis's expression amazed Eliza. "Guess you guys heard. We gotta go home now."

At their outcry, he shrugged. "Can't help it. That's just the way things is. We'll come back tomorrow."

Eliza thought to herself, *Oh, no, you won't.* She kept her opinion quiet, though, saving it until she had a firm grip on Lenny.

"We ain't gettin' outta here with you standin' there," Cletis yelled at his sister. "Go on. I'll be along shortly."

"All right. I'll go, but you'd better follow me home. And the rest of you better go on home, too."

As she talked, Vanda tossed Cletis's pants to the side. What happened next took them all by surprise. Vanda stepped backward, landing on loose rock. Her ankle twisted under her. Her arms flew up as if to embrace the creek, and she fell full length, face forward into the water.

The boys' hoots of laughter as Vanda struggled to right herself released Eliza from her stupor. She rushed to the water's edge, shouting at them to be quiet. "Don't you know Vanda could be hurt?"

She reached her hand toward Vanda. "Here, let me help you out."

Vanda sat in waist-deep water, her clinging skirts draped about her bent knees. Her face flamed as she struggled to her feet. "I can do it."

Eliza asked, "Can you make it to my house?"

At Vanda's nod Eliza turned to the boys, still watching with smirks on their faces. "As soon as we're gone, you get out of there and go home. Do you understand me?"

"We done said we would, didn't we?" Cletis answered for them all.

She turned away, knowing she would have to trust them. Vanda needed her immediate attention, and she wouldn't worry now that she knew where Lenny was.

The three girls set out, walking quietly until they were past the grove of trees. Then a giggle came from Vanda. Eliza looked at her in surprise. Their eyes met, and the merriment in Vanda's expression was contagious.

"I must have looked ridiculous sitting in that water." She grinned.

As Eliza nodded, laughter burst from both girls. Before long all three were laughing hysterically.

As they neared town, Kathrene gained control first. She spoke between giggles, "Honestly, I'm just glad you didn't get hurt."

"So am I." Vanda looked down at her dress. She held it away from her legs as she walked. "I feel stupid. Dunking myself that way." She grew sober. "Maybe I should go on home."

Kathrene shook her head. "It'll be no trouble for you to stop by our house and change."

Eliza led the way upstairs to her room while Kathrene headed for the kitchen to wash the neglected dishes from their meal.

Eliza crossed to the bed and spread the quilt over it. "When we discovered Lenny gone this morning, our housework was forgotten." She apologized for her unmade bed in the otherwise neat room.

"Your house looks wonderful to me." Vanda stood in the middle of the floor. "I'm afraid I may drip on your rug, though."

"Don't worry about it." Eliza opened the door to her wardrobe. She reached for one of the dresses Mary had made, but Vanda stopped her.

"How about this one instead?" Vanda pulled one of Eliza's oldest dresses from the wardrobe.

"Take one of these new ones."

"If I can't wear this one, I won't borrow any." A determined light shone in Vanda's eyes.

"All right, but I don't feel like much of a friend letting you wear that old thing."

"You're the best friend I've ever had, Eliza." Vanda turned away, peeling out of her wet dress.

Eliza laid some underclothes on the bed and reached to take the dress. "Here, I'll hang your clothes outside to dry." She opened the door and started through it when a large yellow and green bruise on Vanda's back caught her eye. Vanda's wet, tangled hair hung down, covering most of it.

She spoke before she thought. "What did you do to your back? It looks like someone took a stick to you."

Vanda looked over her shoulder at Eliza and laughed. "Don't be silly."

"There's a huge bruise on your back."

Vanda appeared to be puzzled. She tried to see her back by twisting around. "Maybe I fell on a rock in the creek."

"Maybe."

Eliza vaguely remembered seeing old bruises on Vanda's face and arms before, but she didn't pursue the subject; because at that moment the downstairs door slammed, and Lenny's voice called out, "I'm home now, and I hope you're satisfied. You just ruined a good afternoon for me."

"Whoa, Fellow, I'd rephrase that if I were you."

Eliza's eyes grew wide as she recognized James's voice. "Your sister's not the one who took off without telling anyone where she was going."

Vanda grabbed up the undergarments and began pulling them on. "Oh, dear. It must be getting late. I've got to get home before Poppa does."

Eliza barely heard her as she traced James's and Lenny's voices going into the kitchen. What was James doing here? Her heart rate increased as she closed the door and moved down the hall to the stairs.

ten

As Eliza carried Vanda's wet dress through the parlor, she saw Lenny curled up on the sofa, already engrossed in a book, munching a slice of bread. James straddled a chair in the kitchen. She didn't look at him, even though she could feel his eyes on her.

She pinned the garments to the clothesline, returned to the house, and walked back across the kitchen. James's voice, mocking, followed her into the parlor.

"Good afternoon, James. Thank you for closing up the shop while you looked for my little lost brother. You can't imagine how much I appreciate it."

Vanda ran down the stairs, her hair in wet ringlets down her back. "Eliza, thank you so much for the loan of this dress. I'll be especially careful with it." She pulled the front door open. "I've got to get home now. Cletis and Poppa will be wanting supper."

Eliza closed the door behind Vanda. She took a deep breath, then pushed the kitchen door open.

Eliza caught the twinkle in his eyes as James grinned at her. She turned away to hide her own smile. "Vanda's gone. She had to hurry home to fix supper for her father."

Kathrene dried her hands and hung the tea towel by the sink. "I guess she found some clothes to wear."

"Yes." Eliza nodded. "She took one of my oldest dresses. I couldn't get her to take a nicer one."

James cleared his throat noisily. Eliza turned to see a wide smile on his face. "Good afternoon, Eliza."

The corners of her mouth twitched. "Good afternoon, James. I've been so busy I haven't had time to tell you how much I appreciate the help you gave us in finding Lenny. I'm sure we couldn't have done it without you."

James stared at her. His smile faded and then came back with a laugh. He stood, shoving the chair under the table. "All right. Maybe I didn't find him, but I looked. When Mr. Leach said you still hadn't found him after dinner, I closed shop and looked everywhere I could think of. I just didn't think of the creek."

Eliza's conscience smote her as she listened to James's deep voice. "I'm sorry, James. I didn't realize. Really, I thank you for being concerned."

"That's all right." He stepped around Eliza to the door. "I'd better get back to work. There are still a few hours left in this day."

He nodded toward Kathrene, his gaze returning to linger on Eliza. "I'll let myself out. Bye, Eliza. Kathrene."

❧

The day Father, Mary, and Nora were due home, Eliza left the dishes to Kathrene while she took the butter churn and a chair from the kitchen to the back porch. Lenny had behaved himself after the creek incident, but first one thing and then another had brought James to their door the last two weeks. First it was milk and now cream. He claimed his cow was giving more than they could use. And twice he had come about shop business. As if Eliza knew anything about making barrels. Mostly they'd just talked about nothing in particular before he went back to work. Eliza smiled, thinking how much she enjoyed his company.

She poured in the cream, dropped the wooden lid in place, and sat with her legs straddling the churn. As she worked, butter slowly emerged from the liquid while her arms grew tired. She lifted the lid to peer inside. Pale yellow clumps floated in the cream. Her butter was done.

She dropped the lid back into place at the sound of a wagon on the road. Her butter forgotten, she hurried from the porch and around the house. Father pulled back on the reins, bringing the wagon to a stop before jumping off to catch Eliza in a bear hug.

He pulled back and looked over her head. "I see the house is still standing."

She acted indignant. "Father, you know I'm quite capable of taking care of things."

He laughed as Kathrene and Lenny rushed from the house. "Why didn't you tell us they were back?" Kathrene admonished Eliza as she brushed past to give Father a quick hug. He then swept Lenny up and hugged him close.

Lenny's wide smile belied his protest. "Hey, I ain't no baby." His thin arms circled his father's neck and squeezed tight.

Mary, holding three-year-old Nora on her lap, watched her husband's homecoming with a smile before calling to him, "I'd like my share of hugs."

Father set Lenny down and reached up to circle her waist with his hands. "I was being selfish, wasn't I?"

"Just a little, but you're forgiven." She smiled down at him. "Why don't you take Nora first? I think Eliza is aching to get hold of her."

Nora was fine when Father handed her to Eliza, but the minute Mary's feet touched the ground, she began struggling to be free. "Mama. I want Mama." Her little arms reached toward Mary.

Eliza felt as if she'd been slapped. "Nora, don't you remember me?" She stroked the little girl's velvety face.

A wail mixed with cries for "Mama" was her answer. Nora's large brown eyes became puddles of distress, filling and overflowing down her cheeks. Nora strained against Eliza's hold, leaning her little body as far as she could toward Mary.

Mary reached for Nora. "I don't know what is the matter with her. It's really hard to tell what little ones are thinking."

Nora snuggled her head against Mary's shoulder and popped her thumb into her mouth.

Eliza saw the look of sympathy on Kathrene's face, and her heart hardened. This wouldn't have happened if she'd been allowed to go with Father.

Mary walked toward the house with Kathrene close beside

her. They disappeared inside while Eliza stood watching.

Father patted Eliza's shoulder as he turned toward the wagon. "Don't worry about Nora. She'll come around. Remember, it's been a long time since she's seen you."

Eliza shrugged from his hand. She didn't want sympathy. She wanted her little sister. She went back to the butter she had left on the porch.

She soon had the butter wrapped and stored in the cellar and the buttermilk in a half-gallon jar ready to drink for breakfast. She was closing the cellar door when Father found her.

"So there you are. I've been looking for you." He grinned at her, slipping his arm around her shoulders. "I was beginning to think you'd disappeared."

She shook her head. "No, just working as usual. Mr. Hurley's cow is suddenly giving more than they can use. I made some butter."

Father laughed, giving her a quick hug. "That's my Eliza. One day you'll make some man a good wife. You're a lot like your mother, you know."

"I am?" Eliza looked up at her father. He couldn't have given her a nicer compliment.

"Yes, you are, more so than either Vickie or Cora." He sat on the back steps. "Here, sit beside me. I have some things to tell you."

Eliza's heart constricted at the serious look on his face. She sat beside him, turning so she could watch his expression as he talked.

His smile gentled, not lighting his face the way it usually did. "I've got letters from the girls for you."

"What's wrong?"

He sighed, looking off to the horizon before he answered. "It's Ben and Esther. On the first day of May, three months ago, they had a little girl. They named her Agnes Danielle. She died before the sun set that same day."

"Oh." The one word rushed out with the air Eliza had been holding. Her eyes filled with tears of sympathy for her brother and his wife. "How terrible."

"Ben and Esther are strong. Their faith in God will see them through."

As she thought of Ben and Esther's loss, her own problems seemed trivial. If they could remain strong, so could she. She brushed at her eyes and stood. "I'm glad you told me. Maybe God will give them another baby."

"Yes, maybe so." Father stood and reached for the back door. "Come on inside, and I'll give you those letters. They wrote to Lenny and Kathrene, too."

Kathrene? Why would they write to her? She walked ahead of her father into the kitchen and took the letters from him. She smiled, holding them close to her heart. "I'll be in my room if you need me."

He grinned. "Don't worry. We won't bother you until you've finished reading."

"Thanks, Father." She reached up on her tiptoes to kiss him on the cheek. "I'm glad you're home." Then she turned and walked toward the parlor. She stopped, her hand on the door. "Father, what about the other two babies? Are they all right?"

"They're as fat and sassy as any two babies I've ever seen."

"And you're not proud of them?" She smiled at the obvious pride on his face.

"Of course I am. Now you get on upstairs and read your letters before I tell you everything that's in them."

Her smile faded when she caught sight of Kathrene on the sofa poring over the letters she had received. She looked up at Eliza, a wide smile on her lips. "You don't know how blessed you are to have sisters. All my life I wanted a sister, and now I have five."

Eliza forced a smile that she didn't feel and ran up the stairs to her room. She fell across her bed. She could hardly wait to read her letters. She placed them all in a neat stack to the side and reached for the first one.

As soon as Eliza opened her letter and saw the carefully

printed script inside, she realized it was not from one of her sisters but from Grace Newkirk.

> *I miss our times together. I have no one to share my secrets with. My biggest news isn't much of a secret. Eliza, I'm going to be married. I wish you could stand with me at our wedding early next spring. I'll be Mrs. Jack Seymour. His family moved in this past spring. He's a wonderful Christian man. He's good, kind, and thoughtful. I know you'd love him, too, if you were here. (But not as much as I do!)*

The ink on the page blurred as Eliza stared at it. So Grace was getting married. A gnawing pain pulled at her stomach.

She rolled over on her back, still clutching Grace's letter. Cora, Esther, and Ivy were all married, and now Grace had found the right man. Even Kathrene, who couldn't cook or keep a neat house, had two men clamoring for her attention.

A long, sad sigh escaped as she rolled back over. She read Esther's letter next. Like the woman who wrote it, it was filled with love and faith in God. Even her heartbreak over the loss of her baby was tempered by her faith.

A paragraph toward the end caught Eliza's eye.

> *Ben and I have been praying about God's will in our lives. We love it here in our cabin with most of our family around us. (You, Father, and Lenny would make our joy complete.) But it seems God is speaking to our hearts that He has work for us to do. Just as Father felt he must move on, so it seems, must we. We have talked to Brother Timothy, and Ben has written to the missionary alliance he recommended. Eliza, we are so excited that God has chosen us to be missionaries to the Indian people in Kansas Territory. We are preparing as much as we can now so we'll be ready to go next spring. From the way it looks now, we will be leaving here right after Grace's wedding. Isn't God good?*

Eliza wiped tears from her eyes. Esther had just suffered the greatest loss a woman can have, yet there was no indication of self-pity in her letter. Instead it was filled with the wonder of God's love and of her desire to give herself to lost people. Eliza felt convicted of her own selfishness and lack of commitment.

She shrugged off the unwelcome mood and picked up Vickie's letter.

Hello, Little Sister, it seems forever since I've seen you. Can you imagine the surprise we all had when Father showed up with a wife? And what a wonderful woman! We fell in love with her immediately. Father said you introduced them. That must mean you love her as much as we do.

It didn't take long to see how much Father cares for her. I don't mean to say he has forgotten Mother. I'm sure he could never do that. But it's obvious this marriage is good for him. I remember how melancholy he was the first few months after Mother died. I worried when you moved to Springfield, not knowing if another location was what he needed. Maybe it wasn't, but Mary obviously is. I wanted to let you know that we all approve of your choice for a stepmother. If we can't have Mother, Mary is certainly our choice, too.

Eliza tossed her sister's letter aside and jumped to her feet. She paced the length of her room and back. How could her sisters welcome another woman into their mother's place? Was she the only one who missed Mother?

She sank to the bed and gathered up Vickie's letter. The rest was about her two rambunctious sons, Nicholas and Christopher. Then she told of her new baby daughter, Faith Victoria.

I was quite ill while I carried this baby. John and I prayed and claimed the promise in Mark 9:23. It says, "If thou canst believe, all things are possible to him that believeth." That's why, when our baby girl was born healthy and strong, we had to name her Faith.

Eliza was glad for the three children Vickie and John had but hoped they didn't have any more. As far as she was concerned, it was not worth the risk of her sister's life. She turned back to her letter.

Oh, yes, I must tell you that both John and I have accepted Jesus as our Savior. Brother Timothy is a powerful speaker and very good at tending to the needs of his congregation. He is a young man without a wife, but he seems to have wisdom beyond his years. It was through his influence that we found our way.

Again, Eliza wiped tears. Her oldest brother, Ben, had been first to accept Christ, and then their mother came to the Lord after Nora's birth. Cora was next. But it took their mother's death to bring Eliza and her father to the Lord. Now John and Vickie had joined their spiritual family. Eliza's heart sang.

Finally, she turned to the last letter—the one from Cora. She skimmed the part that told how much Cora liked Mary. Then Cora told of her new baby. Eliza read carefully.

Eliza, you don't know how much I've missed you. After my baby was born, I thought of you and was sad. My sadness is for both of you because you will not get to watch him grow, and he will not have the benefit of his aunt Eliza's guidance. After all, what better teacher could he have for arguing with his younger brothers and sisters? Could anyone have been better than the two of us, do you think? Truly, I would love to have one of our old verbal fights.

Eliza smiled at her sister's nonsense. She, too, missed the loving rivalry that had gone on between herself and Cora. She turned back to her letter to see what else she could learn about her new nephew.

> *Speaking of disagreements, Aaron and I had our first over our son's name. Can you believe that? For some reason, he wanted the name Jesse. I wanted Dane. Being the submissive wife that I am, I gave in to him. Our son's name is Jesse Dane. Of course, I call him Dane, and even Aaron is beginning to, as well.*

Eliza laughed. She couldn't imagine Aaron disagreeing with Cora about anything. He doted on her and would give in to any whim she had. She sighed. If only she could find a man to love her half as much.

She gathered up her letters and put them in her dresser drawer. She knew in the coming months she would read them over and over, savoring each memory they brought of home and the ones she loved.

That night Nora slept in the downstairs bedroom with Father and Mary. Eliza kept silent about the situation, but inwardly she hurt. Nora treated her like a stranger. She ran to Kathrene and Mary with every need. By the end of the week, Eliza despaired of ever winning her confidence.

Then on Saturday evening after supper, the family relaxed together in the parlor. Father stood at the mantel, watching his wife sew by candlelight. "Why don't you put that down and see if you can win a game of checkers against me?"

Mary smiled up at him. "It's not likely I could do that."

"I'll go easy on you." Father picked up the set. "You'll be putting your eyes out, anyway, doing such close work in this dim light."

Mary lifted the garment and bit off a thread. "I've sewn in dim light for years."

"But you don't have to now." He moved a small table between Mary's chair and the end of the sofa. He opened the board on the table and started putting the pieces in place.

Mary laughed at his persistence. She laid the half-made

• garment aside. "I suppose Nora can wait for her dress."

Nora, who had been quietly playing on the floor with a doll, looked up at her name. She tossed her doll to the side and ran to Mary. "I can play, too."

"Of course, you may, Darling." Mary held her hands out. "Would you like to sit on my lap?"

Nora's shoulder-length hair bounced as she nodded. Eliza bit her lower lip as she watched her little sister. She looked so happy with Mary.

Father leaned back in his chair and tried to look sternly at his little daughter. "All right, you may play, but you wait until Mama tells you what to do."

Nora's big, brown eyes were serious as she nodded. "Yes, Fauver."

They played one game with Nora moving Mary's pieces, and Father won easily.

"See, I told you I couldn't play this game." Mary laughed and gave Nora a hug. "Even with my little helper, I lost."

"You need practice. How about another game?"

Mary shook her head. "I've had all the checkers I want for one night."

Eliza stood. "I'll play with you, Father."

"All right." Father grinned at Mary, teasing her. "Now I'll have some competition."

"No, me play." Nora grabbed a red playing piece in each hand.

Eliza's heart sank, but Mary came to her rescue. "Nora, I know if you talk nice to your sister, she'll let you help, just like I did. Would you like to do that?"

Nora looked from the checkers to Eliza and nodded. Mary stood with her, letting Eliza take her place.

Eliza held her little sister close for a moment. It felt so good to finally hold Nora's warm little body without her squirming for freedom.

Once her sister was secure on her lap, Eliza kept Nora as long as she could. Father won the first game. She found it hard to concentrate with Nora moving the pieces. She lost the second game, but she had two pieces crowned king before Father's kings jumped them.

When she won the third game, Father yawned. "Well, I think we'd better call it a night. Lenny, why don't you hand me my Bible?"

"Are you quitting because you finally lost, Father?" Eliza smiled at him.

He grinned back. "Do you think I'm that childish? No, don't answer." He laughed and took the Bible Lenny handed him. "Let's see what God's Word has for us tonight."

Eliza kept Nora with her throughout family devotions and afterward. She helped her into her nightgown as the family got ready for bed. She even carried her outside to the outhouse.

The sun was just sinking below the western horizon when they returned to the house. Eliza's steps were slow, trying to delay the moment her sister would go back to Mary.

"Nora, how would you like to sleep in my room upstairs tonight?" She tried to keep her voice light, although she felt as if her life depended on the answer.

Nora looked at her older sister. "Where you room?"

"You haven't even seen my room, have you?" Eliza's steps quickened. "How about we go look at it, okay?"

Nora's small head nodded. "Okay."

Eliza carried Nora upstairs without confronting anyone. "It's right in here." She pushed open the door and tossed Nora on her bed so that she bounced.

Nora's happy laughter thrilled her. She scrambled to her feet, her arms lifted. "Do again."

Eliza picked her up and hugged her before positioning her over the bed. "Here goes." She pretended to drop her but didn't.

Nora squealed and grabbed for Eliza's arms. "Do again."

Eliza laughed, this time letting go. Nora fell on the soft bed with a shriek of laughter.

"What's going on in here?" At her father's voice, Eliza turned, lost her balance, and sat down beside Nora.

Nora scrambled up, standing on Eliza's lap, her arms wrapped around her neck. Her lower lip stuck out. "Liza mine."

Father laughed and then slipped his arm around Mary's waist as she came up beside her. He grinned down at her. "It would appear that we've lost a roommate."

Mary's smile widened. "I'm glad to see that you two girls have made up."

Eliza met her soft green eyes and for the moment felt no antagonism. "So am I."

She looked up at her father. "Does that mean Nora can sleep here now?" Her arms tightened around the little girl.

He nodded. "If that's what you want."

"It is." Eliza's smile lit her face. For the first time in a long time, she felt happy.

As if to make up for her earlier behavior, Nora became Eliza's shadow. She sat on her lap all through church the next morning. Eliza kept so busy trying to keep her quiet that she had no idea what the sermon was about.

However, she was well aware of James sitting on the other side of the church with his mother and sister. He added to her happiness when he stopped to talk to her and Nora after church. "I won't ask if you are all right this morning. That sparkle in your eyes tells me you are."

Eliza laughed. "Yes, I'm feeling much better now that my little sister is here."

"I'm glad." James smiled and stepped aside as a couple of young women joined them and exclaimed over Nora. He waved over their heads and said, "I'll see you later."

eleven

Eliza was glad to see Vanda slip into the back pew Sunday evening just before the minister opened his Bible.

" 'Except a man be born again, he cannot see the kingdom of God.' " He paused, stepped to the side of the pulpit, and pointed a finger at the congregation. "Where will you spend eternity?"

Eliza had never heard him talk so fast nor so loud as he paced from one side of the pulpit to the other. She bowed her head and prayed for any who were in need of salvation.

When the altar call was given, Vanda make her way with four others to the front. Mary, Father, and Kathrene went forward to pray with those seeking salvation. Mary knelt beside Vanda.

Eliza held Nora on her lap and made sure Lenny stayed by her side. She felt shaken. She could think of no time she had spoken to Vanda about her soul. She hadn't even considered that Vanda might be in need of salvation.

Tears of repentance for her own neglect trickled down Eliza's cheeks. She bowed her head and prayed, asking God to forgive her for being so selfish with all He had given her.

After church, she waited by the door while Vanda made her way toward her. A wide smile dominated her thin face. Her large brown eyes danced with happiness.

"Oh, Eliza, I'm so glad you waited." The two girls hugged. Vanda pulled back. "Do you know how wonderful I feel right now?"

A flush covered Eliza's face. Had Vanda not known she was a Christian? She nodded. "Yes, I do."

Vanda tugged on Eliza's arm. "Let's step outside. I want to ask you something."

Eliza allowed the other girl to lead her to a tree near the side of the church. It was dark there, away from the lantern light on the front steps.

"Will you pray with me for my father?"

"Your father?"

Vanda looked down with her head bowed. Eliza had to strain to hear her voice. "Poppa is a good man when he isn't drinking. He had so much in Germany, before he came to America. But he's a younger son, and there was no inheritance for him." She looked at Eliza. "He thought he would be successful in America, but every business he tried failed. Then he met my mother. She was young and beautiful, and her family had money. She was a Wingate."

"You mean you're related to Mr. Wingate?" Eliza couldn't keep the surprise from her voice.

Vanda nodded. "Yes, he's my uncle."

"I didn't know."

Vanda smiled. "Trennen works for them, but other than that we don't associate. Poppa's pride won't let us." She seemed impatient to continue as several people came outside. "My parents eloped. In Pennsylvania, Poppa was able to find enough work to keep us alive. Then Uncle Charles came here, and Mama got sick. Poppa would have done anything for her. When she wanted to be near her brother, he packed us up and moved. His heart broke when she died. He won't leave now because she's buried here."

"How sad." Eliza didn't know what to say.

"Eliza, I'm sure you already know the rest." Vanda looked down. "You've seen the bruises. Poppa's always sorry when he's sober, but the drink turns him mean."

Eliza's heart went out to her friend.

She nodded. "Of course, Vanda, I'll pray."

"Thank you, Eliza." She laughed. "I am so happy tonight."

Eliza looked around at the departing congregation. Her father stood on the steps. He shook the minister's hand, then took Mary's arm and stepped off the porch. Nora sat on Mary's other arm as if she belonged there. "Vanda, you aren't going to walk home in the dark, are you? Why don't you come with us? I'm sure Father won't mind taking you home."

"Thank you, but I have a ride." Vanda smiled and indicated some young men standing in a group several yards away.

As Eliza looked, James Hurley separated himself from the others and came toward them. "It won't be out of James's way to take me, but I do appreciate your offer."

"Good evening, Eliza." James smiled.

"Hello, James."

He nodded. "Well, Vanda, are you ready to go?"

"Yes." Vanda took his offered arm. Eliza watched them walk toward his wagon. Her heart wrenched at the sight, and she realized she cared for James more than she should.

⁂

One day in late September, Kathrene came home with news of a taffy pull. "It's at Barbara Martin's house." Her eyes sparkled in excitement. "Charles asked me to go with him."

Mary looked up. "That's wonderful, Dear. When is it?"

"This Saturday evening." Kathrene moved to stand next to Eliza. "Barbara said to tell you to come, too, Eliza. If you'd like, you may ride over with Charles and me. He said to be sure and ask you."

Eliza's rolling pin stopped in midstroke. She looked up at Kathrene, her brown eyes snapping. "Thank you, Kathrene, but if I go, I'll go by myself."

"Eliza," Kathrene spoke softly, pleading, "we really want you with us."

Eliza shook her head. "I don't think that would be wise." She lifted her pie dough and placed it carefully on the pan.

"Eliza, do we have any leavening?" Mary stood at the cabinet rummaging through the baking supplies.

"I thought there was some."

"Well, there isn't now." Mary turned and smiled. "Would you two girls mind running to the store?"

Eliza wondered if Mary asked them both to go in an effort to bring them together again. She felt the prick of her conscience as she realized that most of the problem was her fault. Walking to town with Kathrene was the least she could do to make amends.

They had just started down the road toward town when Eliza heard footsteps behind them.

"Hey, wait up, will you?"

"What do you want?" Eliza asked Lenny as he caught up with them.

"Ma, er. . ." He glanced quickly at Eliza. "Mary said I could go with you."

"All right." Eliza pointed her finger at him. "But you behave yourself. You either stay with us or go to Father's shop. Do you understand?"

He nodded. "I'm goin' to Father's."

After the girls left the store, they started across the square to Father's shops.

"Miss Kowski, wait a minute."

They both turned to see Stephen Doran hurrying toward them. Eliza stepped back, frowning at Kathrene's sharp intake of breath. Was she really so smitten by this penniless drifter?

"Miss Kowski." He smiled, and Eliza had to admit he was very good-looking. "I understand Miss Barbara Martin is having a taffy pull this Saturday evening. I would be honored if you would go with me."

"Oh, I can't."

Eliza smiled at the expression on Kathrene's face.

"If it's because I'm a stranger to your folks, I'd be glad to talk to your father. . .or mother." His expression was as woebegone as hers.

"No, it isn't that." Kathrene shook her head. "I've already promised someone else."

"Then you are going?"

"Yes, I'll be there."

"Well." He jammed his hands in his pockets. "I'll see you then." Again he smiled at her. "Until Saturday."

As soon as he left, Kathrene said, "Oh, I didn't think. Why didn't I suggest he take you?"

Eliza gasped. "Don't you dare! I don't need your charity. I'm going to see my father now. I'll come home later with Lenny."

How dare Kathrene patronize her just because she had two young men at her beck and call while Eliza had none? Tears stung her eyes, and she wiped at them as she neared the door to the chandler shop.

Father was alone in the shop when she entered. He looked up from the ledger he had been working on and smiled at her. "What a sight for sore eyes."

She smiled. "Is Lenny here? I thought I'd walk home with him."

"He's in the back. I thought he might as well do a little work before school starts again."

Eliza moved to a display of candles hanging from the ceiling and tapped at them, watching them swing back and forth.

"Why don't you tell me what the problem is?"

She tried to laugh, but it came out as a sob. "Can't I hide anything from you?"

He pulled her around to face him, his hands on her shoulders. "I know you haven't been happy. Please, tell me what it is."

"It's so silly." At her hiccupy laugh, he pulled her against his chest, and she couldn't hold the tears back.

While his shirt grew damp, she told him of the party. "Kathrene has two beaux. I don't have anyone. I'm almost twenty."

He patted her back. "Maybe it just isn't God's time yet, or maybe it is, and you haven't recognized it."

"What do you mean by that?" She looked up at him as he handed her his handkerchief.

A jingle at the door warned them that someone was coming. He pushed her gently toward the workroom. "You step in there just a minute until I take care of our customer."

Eliza stood in the workroom, trying to repair the damage to her face with her father's handkerchief. Two large vats sat in the middle of the room. Candle wax and rolls of wick waited on the floor. Finished candles lay in piles on a table. Lenny was nowhere to be seen.

After what seemed a long time, Eliza carefully opened the door to the shop a crack. She couldn't hear anyone talking. She pushed it open a little farther. She didn't see anyone. As she pushed the door all the way open and stepped into the shop, Father came in the front door.

He grinned. "Oops! I got caught, didn't I? Sorry to keep you waiting, but I had to take care of some business next door."

"That's all right, Father. I need to go home, anyway."

He lifted her chin and gave her a quick kiss on the forehead. "Don't look so sad. Maybe things aren't as bad as they seem."

She smiled for his benefit. "Maybe not."

She hadn't gotten more than a hundred yards from the shops on her way home when quick footsteps sounded behind her. Thinking it was Lenny, she stopped and turned around.

James came within an inch of running into her. "What'd you stop so quick for?"

"I thought you were my brother." She stepped back to put some distance between them.

"No, I'm not your brother." The look on his face and the inflection in his voice caused a flush to spread across her cheeks. "I was trying to catch up with you so I could ask you if you're going to the taffy pull Saturday night at the Martins'."

She looked down. "I planned to, but I don't see what business it is of yours."

He threw his hands out in a helpless gesture. "Eliza Jackson, you are the most aggravating woman I've ever dealt with."

"Oh, and I suppose you've dealt with a lot of women?" She turned a saucy face to him.

His gray eyes twinkled above a grin that set her pulse racing. "Not so many you need be concerned."

"And who says I'm concerned about what you do?"

"Eliza." He grew serious. "All I want is for you to go with me to the party. How about it? Can we call a truce and go as friends?"

She nodded, surprised that her voice sounded so normal. "I suppose it would be all right. I should ask my father first."

James smiled. "Good. I'll be at your house around six thirty." He turned and walked back toward town, whistling.

❧

The promise of winter brought crispness to the September air Saturday evening as Eliza left the house with James.

They walked down the steps toward the road. Eliza noticed the absence of any vehicle in front. She glanced up at James as he took her elbow to help her over a wagon rut.

"You realize, of course, that Kathrene left ten minutes ago in a shiny blue Victoria pulled by a matched set of horses."

"My, a blue one, even." Knowing James, she assumed he was making fun of her.

"Yes. Cobalt blue with matching Morocco upholstery."

"Now, I am impressed. First the horses and now the upholstery. Everything must match." He grinned down at her. "What did you do? Come out and inspect it?"

He was making fun of her. She fell into his mood. "Why not? I'm not so lucky as Kathrene. I suppose I shall always have to walk wherever I go, unless I can somehow take Charles from Kathrene. He's the only man I know who can afford such luxury."

"And what's wrong with walking?" A frown set on James's face. "The night is warm enough, there's a full moon overhead, and we're both young and able."

Eliza looked up at James. She had been joking, but by an instinct peculiar to women, she knew that in his mind the joke had turned to criticism.

"There's not a thing wrong with walking. Actually, I quite enjoy it."

She smiled at him and was glad to see his frown disappear.

The Martin house blazed with lights. Just before they went inside, James said, "Your father would have more business than he could handle if there were more parties like this one."

Eliza laughed. "I think you're right. They must have every candle in the house burning and a few lanterns as well."

Barbara opened the door at their knock. "Come on in. Make yourselves at home." She pointed toward a door off the parlor. "Pile your wraps on the bed in there."

James and Eliza shared a smile as she fluttered off to attend to someone's call. They tossed their outer garments on the bed and returned to the parlor just as Vanda came in, followed by her older brother.

Trennen nodded at James. When he turned to Eliza, a flush touched her cheeks at his scrutiny.

James's hand closed gently around her upper arm. "Come on, it sounds like they're starting the candy."

"Vanda." Eliza motioned toward her friend. "We don't want to miss out on the taffy pulling, do we?"

"We sure don't." Vanda smiled and joined them as they followed Trennen into the kitchen.

"Come on, everyone, it's just about ready." Barbara bustled about the large kitchen, setting out plates and butter for each of her guests. "This is going to be so much fun." She handed Eliza a plate.

"Hey, don't I get one?" James asked.

"Sorry, just one to a couple." Barbara turned to Vanda. "Here's your plate, but who's your partner? You don't want to pull with your brother. I know. Why don't you take mine?"

Before Vanda could answer, Barbara ran across the room and grabbed her brother's arm. He was talking to the Ross boys and resisted at first.

"I wish she wouldn't do that." Vanda looked embarrassed.

"Don't you like her brother?" Eliza asked.

"It isn't that. Joe's fine. But he doesn't look like he wants to come."

"I wouldn't be so sure about that." Eliza nudged her friend as Joe straightened and looked across the room. His frown of annoyance was replaced by a smile as he met Vanda's eyes. He nodded and followed his sister.

Joe Martin was at least six feet tall and thin. His hair, a dark brown, contrasted with his fair sister's. Eliza had never thought of him as anything more than Barbara's brother. Now she watched Vanda's face as he approached and wondered if the two of them might make a good couple.

She glanced across the room and caught Trennen's gaze on her. A slow, lazy smile crossed his face, and she looked quickly away.

She was glad when Barbara's mother lifted a large spoonful of candy from the pan and watched it sheet off. A sweet aroma filled the air. "The taffy's ready."

A chorus of cheers greeted her pronouncement. Eliza and James got into line with the other couples to get their plate of hot taffy. The atmosphere was festive and loud with everyone laughing and talking while they waited for the candy to cool enough to handle.

She avoided Kathrene and Charles as much as she could, but she noticed that Stephen Doran stayed close to them. He had come alone, and Barbara had agreed to be his partner, though Eliza knew she would have preferred David Ross.

Finally, someone decided the candy had cooled enough. James reached into the bowl and scooped off some butter. He inclined his head toward the only empty corner left at the moment. "Come on, Eliza, and bring the plate of candy."

"Yes, Sir." She followed him, ignoring his raised eyebrows.

"Set the plate down and take my hands." He spread the butter over his own hands and then reached for hers.

"As you wish, Sir." She set the plate down and started to stretch her hands toward his, but the look on his face stopped her.

"If you don't stop calling me *sir*. . ." If he had finished his sentence, she was sure she wouldn't have heard it for the pounding of her heart.

Her voice sounded small even to herself as she said, "James."

He grinned. "That's much better." He took her hands then and rubbed them between his own.

"There, that should be good enough." Their eyes met, and warmth radiated between them. James dropped her hands and reached for the plate.

As they pulled the candy between them, it stretched and hardened. Barbara told them to make some thin, ropelike strands for a game they would be playing.

"All right, everyone listen, and I'll explain the game to you." Barbara clapped her hands for attention.

She held up a large bowl. "Break off a piece of your rope candy about one to two inches long. Put it in this bowl, and then we'll pick someone to start the game."

"Aren't you going to tell us how to play first?" someone called.

Barbara's long blond ringlets swished across her back as she shook her head. "I won't have to. You'll know soon enough."

The bowl made the rounds of the room and came back almost full. Barbara giggled. "If we use all this, we may be here all night. Who wants to go first?"

"Why don't you go first and show us how?" Joe spoke from the corner. Several others voiced their agreement.

"All right, but I'll need a partner." Barbara turned to smile at David Ross. "I choose you, David."

David had brought a girl named Anna Johnson whom Eliza didn't know. He joined Barbara in the center of the room near the long trestle table. "Okay, what do I do?"

Barbara reached into the bowl and withdrew a piece of the short candy. "You remember this game, don't you, David? We played it before." She clamped one end of the candy with her teeth, her lips making an O around it. She then bent toward David with her hands clasped behind her back.

David grinned. "Sure, I remember." He put his hands behind his back and bent toward her. His mouth closed around the candy, and he bit it off, then straightened, chewing the piece in his mouth.

He grinned at the others and swept a bow amid laughter and

hand clapping. As he straightened, he said, "All right, it's my turn now since I bit it in two." His eyes glanced about the room, settling on Anna. "Will you accept my challenge, Anna?"

Anna's face grew rosy, and she shook her head, a self-conscious smile on her lips.

"Come on, Anna, it's all in fun."

Anna allowed herself to be cajoled into playing. Her face was bright red by the time David again bit the candy off.

Since the same couple was not allowed to break the candy twice in a row, David chose Barbara next. When she broke the candy, she picked Stephen Doran. Eliza watched him bite the candy and then turn with a gleam in his eye toward Kathrene.

Kathrene's eyes sparkled as she placed her lips around the candy and they touched Stephen's. Eliza silently and slowly counted to five before she heard the snap of the candy in the quiet room. Kathrene picked Charles next, and on it went until it was Trennen's turn.

He turned slowly, his eyes taking in each girl until they rested on Eliza. He cocked his head to one side, his left eyebrow lifting slightly. "Well, come on."

Eliza's heart thudded in her chest. Trennen's good looks and confidence frightened and excited her. She leaned forward, taking the end of the candy in her teeth. Trennen's face was so close to her own. She looked down at the candy. Her vision blurred, and she became conscious of the many watchful eyes surrounding her.

Then Trennen's lips moved forward, across the fraction of an inch that separated them, and touched hers. She jerked back, and the candy broke off in her mouth.

Her face flamed as Trennen whispered, "That was nice. Let's try it again sometime."

"All right, Eliza. Pick another partner," Barbara called to her.

Eliza pointed at James. "I'll challenge you."

His grin showed his acceptance.

Again, Eliza's heart pounded. She picked the longest piece of candy that she could find and clamped the end in her teeth. With her hands clasped behind her back, she leaned toward him. The room grew quiet as he took the other end in his teeth.

Seconds ticked off as they stood, nose to nose, holding the candy. Then it snapped off in James's teeth. His eyes danced at her surprised expression. Their lips had not touched.

After a couple more games, Barbara stood up. "It's getting late, but I want to thank you all so much for coming. I don't know about you, but I've had lots of fun."

Kathrene caught Eliza and James as they put on their wraps. "Charles is bringing the buggy around. Would you like to ride home with us?"

James shrugged. "That's up to Eliza."

She thought of the plush Victoria and was tempted. But then she looked at James and shook her head. "We'll go home the same way we came."

Kathrene shrugged. "All right, if that's what you want."

"It is." James took Eliza's arm and guided her out the door.

They walked together, talking about the party, the town that was growing up around them, and James's plans for his life's work. Before she realized it, they had turned into her front yard.

"I like farming and hope to never live in town, but I also enjoy working with your father."

"So what are you going to do? Be a farmer or a cooper?"

"Both." James grinned down at her as they neared her house. "Unless your father runs me off for keeping you out too late. You know we'd have been here a lot sooner in that fancy blue Victoria."

She nodded as they stopped just short of the front porch. "I know, but it wouldn't have been as much fun."

"So you think walking is fun."

"Depending on the company."

He grinned and then became serious. "Eliza, I enjoyed this

evening very much. So much that I hate to see it end." He searched her face. "Would you consider going with me next Saturday to see my farm? I'd really like to show it to you."

She smiled up at him. "Do I have to walk?"

He laughed. "I don't know. Do you think your father would loan me his buggy?"

"I don't imagine he'll say much against it. If he does, I might put in a good word for you."

James stepped closer, his hands on each of her elbows. "Does that mean you'll go?"

She nodded, unable to speak with him so near.

He leaned toward her. "Eliza, may I kiss you good night?"

Her heartbeat drummed in her ears. Without a word, she nodded.

As he pulled her into his arms and his lips lowered over hers, moisture came unbidden to her eyes. She had not expected such strong feelings to come with a simple kiss.

James smiled down at her. "You'd better go in before your father comes out."

Eliza walked into the house in a daze.

twelve

The next morning at church, Eliza cast shy glances at James. He returned her smiles and after the service went out of his way to speak to her.

"I told my mother I was bringing you out next Saturday."

"I hope it's all right with her."

He smiled. "She's anxious to get acquainted with you. Now all I have to do is get your father's permission."

"Oh, no, you don't." She gave him a saucy grin. "I already asked, and he said yes."

James laughed. "Great, now I know what his answer will be tomorrow when I ask for the use of his buggy."

Lenny ran by, yelling over his shoulder, "Come on, Eliza. Father and Mama are ready to go."

Eliza frowned after him. "I can't believe he calls her 'Mama.' He just does it because Nora does. But Nora doesn't remember Mother."

"Perhaps you shouldn't be so hard on him. He's young, too, you know."

"Maybe." Eliza turned back to him with a smile. "Well, I've got to be going. I'll see you later."

Monday evening Father told Eliza he'd been approached by James and had given him permission to borrow his buggy on Saturday. He grinned at her with a teasing light in his eyes. "I always heard tell a boy was getting serious when he took his best girl out to meet his mother."

Eliza's face flamed. "Don't get your hopes up yet, Father. I'm afraid James just wants to show off his farm. It looks like you're stuck with me for awhile."

Father laughed, but Mary said, "I can't imagine a nicer thing than to have you right here with us always."

Eliza turned toward the stairs without responding.

On Saturday afternoon, the air felt cool while sunshine brought the trees alive with color as Eliza and James rode toward his farm.

They hadn't gone far when he pointed to the left. "This is the north boundary. I've only added twenty acres since my father died. Someday, I'd like to have at least two hundred."

"That would make a nice-sized farm for this part of the country," Eliza said. "What do you raise? Cows, horses, pigs?"

He grinned at her. "Yes."

"Yes! You mean you have all of those?"

"All of those plus chickens, dogs, and cats."

"My, you do have quite a farm." Eliza laughed with him.

He pointed at a house sitting to the left of the road. "Here we are."

Someone had built onto the original log cabin, making a nice-sized house. It stood two stories tall with a fresh coat of whitewash. A dog curled up on the back steps wagged his tail as they walked toward him. He lifted his head, gave one sniff, and then settled back to complete his nap.

"He's not the best watchdog, but he's friendly." James patted the dog's head before opening the door for Eliza.

She laughed and stepped inside.

Mrs. Hurley took a pan of cookies from the oven. She smiled. "I thought you might like a warm treat. There's hot chocolate on the stove." She turned to her daughter. "Pour some out for each of us, Melissa. We'll sit here around the table and visit a spell."

"That sounds nice," Eliza said.

"How is your family, Eliza?" Mrs. Hurley placed the cookies on the table, then pulled a chair out.

James reached for another chair and pulled it from the table for Eliza. She smiled her thanks and then answered his mother. "They're just fine, thank you."

Eliza enjoyed the time she spent with James's mother and sister. Both made her feel at home as they talked about the weather, the town, and their farm. Eliza learned that the farm had been given to James at his father's death more than ten years ago. She was amazed that a boy so young would be trusted with such an undertaking. His mother assured her that he had proven himself worthy, getting up before light to care for the animals and do chores.

Pride set on her face as she smiled at her son. "He worked morning and night to make a living for us and still kept up with his studies. I worried that he couldn't do it with all the responsibilities he had, but James stayed in school until he knew as much as the schoolmaster." She smiled at him.

Eliza looked at James with shining eyes.

He laughed. "Don't let my mother fool you. I have a well-used fishing rod out in the barn to prove I didn't work all the time."

Mrs. Hurley laughed and patted James's hand. "Yes, all boys must play, or they don't make good men."

"Come on, Eliza." James set his mug down. "Let's go look around."

He grasped her hand, pulling her to her feet. She felt self-conscious when he kept her hand firmly in his as they went out the kitchen door.

Together they walked across his farm as he pointed out the various animals and crops. They were walking back toward the house when he pulled her behind a toolshed.

"What's the matter?" She grabbed her bonnet to keep it from slipping off her head.

He turned to face her. His eyes were dark as they looked deep into hers. "There's something I need to know."

She felt as if she couldn't breathe. "What is it?"

His hand touched her neck while his thumb stroked her cheek. "I want to know. . ." He paused a moment as his gaze dropped to her lips. "If I have to ask every time I want to kiss you."

Her heart thudded. She could not speak. All she could do was shake her head from side to side.

"Good." His hand cupped her chin, lifting it until their lips touched. Eliza responded as she hadn't the first time and experienced emotions beyond anything she had ever imagined.

When he pulled away, a grin set on his lips. "You know I plan to take advantage of this, don't you?"

"What do you mean?" Her breath came in short, quick spurts.

"I mean there's still that big tree between us and the house." He stepped around the corner of the toolshed, pointing to an old oak broad enough to hide the two of them from anyone looking out a window.

She walked past him, putting a little distance between them before she spoke. With her head tilted toward one side, she smiled. "That's true, but you'll have to catch me first."

Before the last word left her mouth, she was running as fast as she could toward the house. When she heard the pounding of his feet behind her, an unreasonable alarm gave her the impetus she needed to make it past the tree before he caught her.

He wrapped his arm around her and pulled her close to his side as they continued to the house. He grinned at her struggles to pull away. "If you think you're going to get away from me after that trick, you'd better think again."

"What will your mother think if she sees you holding me this way?"

"Probably that she raised her son to be as smart as she thinks he is." James laughed but removed his arm from her shoulders to hold her hand instead. He stopped at the back steps. "Your father may be worried about me keeping his horse and buggy out too late. I'd better get it back to him."

"What about his daughter?" Eliza pretended to be deeply hurt. "You men always put your possessions above us womenfolk."

"But, Eliza. . ." The twinkle in James's eyes gave away his serious expression. "Don't you know you womenfolk are our possessions, too?"

"You may consider your wife a possession, Mr. Hurley—if you ever find someone who will marry you—but I will never be any man's possession." Eliza lifted her chin defiantly.

James laughed. "That's one statement I can believe, Miss

Jackson." He pulled her toward the door. "Come inside for just a minute; then I'll take you home."

Eliza sat close beside James on the way back to town. She scarcely knew what to think of the new emotions that he had awakened in her.

"You know, I just thought of something." James interrupted her thoughts. "We haven't had a good argument since before Barbara's party."

"It's rather nice, don't you think?"

He grinned at her. "Just being with you is nice."

Her face flushed, and she looked away. As she did, she saw a lone figure trudging toward town ahead of them.

"James, isn't that Vanda?" As they got closer, she gripped his arm. "It is. Please stop and let's give her a ride into town."

Vanda climbed into the back and leaned against the seat. "This is much better than walking."

"Where were you headed?" Eliza asked.

"I need to go to the general store, but my main reason for coming into town was to see you."

"Is something wrong?"

"I think so." Vanda looked to the countryside as it rolled by. "Before I was a Christian, I might have overlooked this, but now I realize how important it is that everyone comes to know the Lord in a personal way."

She looked at Eliza. "I'm concerned about Cletis and Lenny. They are young, but they're doing things they shouldn't, and I'm afraid it'll just get worse as they get older."

Eliza felt a sinking sensation in her middle. What had Lenny done now?

Vanda continued. "I thought you might tell your father that I caught Cletis and Lenny chewing tobacco the other day out behind our outhouse."

"Lenny was at your place?" Eliza was as shocked by that bit of news as she was at what he had been doing.

"Yes, he's been out several times. Cletis knows when Poppa isn't going to be there. The boys said it was all right with your folks."

Eliza sat in stunned silence. It seemed she had quite a bit to talk over with her brother when she got home.

❦

Eliza saw her opportunity to talk to Lenny the next day when he went to the outhouse right after the family returned home from church. She waited until he came out. "I had a talk with Vanda yesterday."

Lenny just looked at her.

"She says she caught you and Cletis with some tobacco. Is that true?"

"So what if it is?" He glared at her. "You ain't my boss."

"I may not be your boss, but I could sure tell Father that Cletis is a bad influence on you. How would you like that?"

She saw fear come into his eyes and then change into something else. But she was unprepared for his next words.

"I guess you got reason to be jealous of me and my friends, 'cause Father don't have to get me no friends."

"What do you mean?"

"Father got you James, didn't he?" Lenny sneered. "I was in the cooper shop when he told James to ask you to that party. James didn't want to, either. He said he didn't think you'd go with him. But Father said he'd sure appreciate it if he'd try, anyhow, so James said he would."

Lenny's voice pounded in Eliza's head as a drum that would not stop. Never in her life had she felt so humiliated and hurt.

Eliza spent the rest of the afternoon in her room. James had told her he wanted to continue working as a cooper. Well, he had certainly earned that right. She reached for her pillow and buried her face in it as great sobs racked her body.

❦

Before church that evening, Eliza crawled into bed and went to sleep. The grief she suffered robbed her natural coloring, leaving her pale. It was not hard, when Kathrene came to wake her, to convince her and then Father that she would be unable to attend the service with them.

As soon as the door closed, she looked to be sure everyone had left her room before she threw the covers back and sat up, clutching her knees to her chest.

Her pride had been deeply wounded, but she couldn't hide away forever while James laughed at her. She would show him and Father, too.

❧

Trennen came to church the following Sunday morning. Although he sat quietly in the pew behind her, Eliza was aware of his presence almost as much as she was aware of James sitting across the church beside his mother and sister.

Before James could reach her, she left the building, and Trennen fell into place behind her. Without touching her, he leaned forward slightly to speak close to her ear. "Good morning, Eliza."

She turned around with a smile. "Good morning, Trennen. It's nice seeing you in church."

She was not the only one glad to see him there. Several stopped to shake his hand. Eliza stayed with him. She saw James heading their way, so she tugged Trennen's sleeve. He went with her without question. James caught up with them before they'd gone far.

"Eliza, could I talk with you?"

"If you have a question about your work, my father is over there." She inclined her head, refusing to look at James. "Now, if you'll excuse me, I'll continue my conversation with Trennen."

She turned away, pulling Trennen with her. James did not follow. Trennen looked down at her, a lazy grin in place. "I might've come to church before now if I'd known everyone wanted me to."

"Of course, everyone wants you to come." Eliza turned to look up at him and saw James join his mother.

"I suppose that's why no one ever asked me."

Eliza looked up at Trennen. "Do you mean the Wingates never asked you?"

"Well, yeah, but they don't count. Vanda, too, but that doesn't mean anything."

"Why not?" Eliza suddenly realized his sister hadn't been

at church. "Where is Vanda, anyway?"

"Probably home with Pop." Trennen shrugged. "I think he was supposed to come in this weekend."

Eliza's eyes widened as she remembered what Vanda had said about her father beating her and Cletis when he came home drunk. Was it possible that she was suffering at her father's hand right now?

Trennen touched her shoulder, bringing her attention back to him. "I'll walk you home."

"I'd have to ask my father first."

"I'll go with you." Trennen took her arm, and together they caught Father and Mary as they headed toward their buggy.

"Father, would it be all right if Trennen walked me home?" Eliza looked hopefully at her father.

He hesitated, looking first at Trennen and then at Eliza. "I suppose if you come straight home, it will be all right."

Trennen nodded. "Thank you, Sir."

Trennen took her hand and placed it in the crook of his arm. Together they crossed the churchyard and started across the road just as James's wagon pulled out in front of them.

Eliza pushed James from her mind and tried to concentrate on the young man beside her. As they came up to the front porch, he stepped back.

"Why don't you come inside for awhile?"

He stuck his hands in his pockets. "Naw, I'd better not, but I'd like to see you again. How about tonight? Do you go to church at night, too?"

She smiled. "Yes, we usually do."

"Good. Then I'll see you there." With that, he turned and walked away.

From then on Trennen never missed a church service, and several times he walked Eliza home. She knew the people were pleased to see him. Many prayed for his salvation, hoping at each altar call that he would be the next to go forward. Eliza also prayed for him, but mostly she enjoyed having a young man interested in her because he liked her and not because he was afraid he'd lose his job.

James tried several times to talk to Eliza, but each time she managed to avoid him.

For awhile Eliza enjoyed Trennen's attention, but as the weeks went by she grew tired of his insincere compliments and chivalrous behavior. At first she pushed her discontent aside, but it would not leave. One Sunday morning she decided she would tell him she no longer wished to see him.

As usual, he sat in the row behind her. When church dismissed, he waited outside for her.

Lately, Father had not been as free with his permission for her to walk out with Trennen as he had at first. So she pulled her father aside. "Father, if Trennen asks to walk me home this morning, may I please? I'd really like to talk to him."

A frown creased Father's forehead. "I don't know, Eliza."

"Father, he's been a perfect gentleman."

"I'm sure that's true. But do you think his sudden interest in attending the house of God has anything to do with his concern for his soul, or is it the attraction he feels for one of God's children?"

Trennen had told Eliza that he started coming to church when he did because he enjoyed the kiss they had shared at the party so much. She flushed as she evaded her father's question. "I can't read his thoughts, Father."

Father sighed. "All right. Go ahead, but be careful."

"Don't worry. I'll be fine." She brushed off his concern. "We're just walking across town."

Before she made it to the back door, James blocked her path. "Eliza, could I talk to you?"

His eyes were dark gray as he looked down at her, his expression serious. She skirted around him. "I'm sorry, Mr. Hurley, but my *unpaid* escort is waiting for me. My father handles any problems with his businesses." She rushed past before he could stop her.

She waved at Trennen and walked toward him, wondering if James was watching.

Trennen smiled when he saw her. "May I walk you home?"

She nodded. "Yes, I've already asked Father, and he said it

was all right. I wanted to talk to you."

When they were out of sight of the churchyard, he reached for her hand. She reluctantly curled her fingers around his.

Trennen squeezed her hand. "I thought you wanted to talk to me. You haven't said more than two words."

Eliza realized that they had already crossed the square downtown. If she were going to get this done, she'd have to do it now.

Her steps slowed. "Trennen, I'm flattered by the attention you've paid me. I enjoy our walks very much. But. . ."

His hand stiffened in hers.

"But I wonder if there isn't someone else you'd rather be with."

He laughed. "Are you jealous?"

"No." She looked quickly at him. "No, I didn't mean that."

His hand squeezed hers again. She winced at the pain, but he as quickly released her hand and, stopping in the road, turned to face her. "Are you wanting another man's attentions? Maybe Hurley?"

The anger in his voice and on his face surprised her. She shook her head. "No, that's not what I meant." How could she explain it to him? What could she say that wouldn't hurt him?

"Good. Then there's nothing to talk about." He took her hand again and continued walking.

They soon reached her front door, and she had accomplished nothing. Before he left, she tried again. "Trennen, I didn't mean to hurt your feelings."

As she hesitated, the front door opened, framing Kathrene. "Eliza, Mother says for you to invite Trennen in to eat with us. She says it's about time the family became acquainted with him."

Trennen's lazy smile softened his blue eyes as he looked down at Eliza. "Well, do I get to stay?"

thirteen

That night when Eliza went to bed, she pulled the covers up to her chin. Trennen had been the most gallant, attentive guest she had ever seen. He'd complimented Mary on her cooking so many times Eliza had felt like gagging. That was one of the problems with him. He said all the right things so often that she questioned his sincerity.

She sighed. How was she going to stop seeing Trennen? Even Father said that he seemed to be a nice young man.

Just thinking about it made her thirsty. She threw the covers back, climbed from bed, and went downstairs to the kitchen.

"Kathrene seemed quite pleased, didn't she?" The muffled voice of her father came from his bedroom.

With her ear near the door, she was able to hear Mary. "I hope we did the right thing."

Father said, "I've heard nothing but good about the boy. I know he's closemouthed about his past, but I think he's everything he claims to be."

"I suppose."

Eliza realized they meant Stephen Doran.

Father said, "I wouldn't be surprised if this isn't the man Kathrene marries."

"You know, Orval, I love all our children. Yours and mine. Vickie and Cora are so sweet. And Ben. How could I help loving him? He's just like his father."

Mary paused for a moment. "Then there's Eliza. I think I began loving her when she walked into my house with that bundle of fabric that was almost as big as she is."

Eliza heard a muffled sob and Father say, "It's all right, Mary. Eliza's a good girl. She'll come around."

"I know." Mary cleared her throat.

"You're a good mother, Mary. You're good with Lenny, and Nora adores you. I'm proud of the way she took to you so quickly." He laughed softly. "And now God is blessing us with one that won't have to adjust to a new mother or a new father."

"Yes." Eliza could hear the smile in Mary's voice. "Our own little one to raise together. I know our baby won't be here until spring, but I get so anxious. I want to know what our child will look like."

Eliza's father spoke, but she didn't hear. How could this be? Surely Mary and Father were not expecting a baby. They couldn't be. Mary was supposed to cook and clean for him. She was not supposed to bear his children.

Eliza crept back to her room, her thirst forgotten.

‮❧‬

As November gave way to December, Eliza's worries grew. Mary's condition became more pronounced, and Trennen refused to leave her alone. Several times she tried to tell him that she didn't want his company anymore, but he refused to listen. And James stopped trying to talk to her.

Eliza didn't feel the freedom to tell her father that she didn't want to go with Trennen. So he gave permission for her to ride to the Christmas play with Trennen, just as he did for Kathrene to ride in Stephen Doran's well-worn buggy.

When the parts for the play were given out, Vanda was chosen to play Mary, the mother of Jesus. Her eyes shone as she turned to Eliza, "Poppa's away working. He said he'd be gone all month, and I hope he is because he would be angry if he knew what I'm doing."

"You mean he wouldn't want you in the play?" Eliza couldn't understand his problem.

Vanda nodded. "He doesn't want us going to church. Cletis comes out of rebellion, but I come because Jesus is my Lord. I can't turn my back on Him."

That evening when Trennen took Eliza home, he walked

her to the door while Vanda and Cletis waited in the Wingates' buggy. In the two months they had been keeping company, Trennen had never done more than hold her hand. Now he stepped up on the porch with her and pulled her into a shadowy corner away from prying eyes. Eliza's heart pounded.

"Trennen, please. . ."

"I love you, Eliza." He stopped her protest, pulling her close to him. "All I want is one kiss."

When she resisted, he pleaded with her. "Don't you love me?"

All the time he talked, he held her close, his cheek against hers. Finally, his lips touched hers, and she felt she had no choice but to surrender. Maybe if she allowed him one kiss, he would let her go.

But Trennen's kiss deepened into something Eliza didn't understand. She shoved against him. "Trennen, no. . ."

"I love you, Eliza." He reached for her again.

"You can't do this, Trennen. It isn't right." Her heart pounded in fear.

She shoved him backward, making him stumble against the porch post. "I want you to leave, Trennen. And I don't want to ride home with you anymore."

He started toward her, a look of anger on his face. Then his expression changed, and his head bowed. "I'm sorry, Eliza. It's just that I love you so much. Don't tell me I can't ever see you again."

Eliza's heart began a hard steady beat. Her head felt light. She watched him standing dejected, and sympathy replaced anger and fear.

"I have to go inside now, Trennen. I'll see you later." She turned and let herself into the house.

❧

Eight days before the Christmas program, Trennen again asked her to let him take her home.

At first she said no.

"Are you afraid of me, Eliza?" Trennen looked sad.

She shook her head. "No, of course not. But I need to go. Father's waiting. He said they are working late on an order tonight so he needs to get back to the shop."

As she turned away, Trennen captured her arm in his hand. "Eliza, I need to talk to you. It's important." He pleaded with her. "I promise you, if you'll go with me tonight, I'll leave you alone from now on if that's what you really want."

She stood looking at him for several seconds, trying to decide what she should do. She didn't love Trennen, and she knew she never would. She loved only one man.

Pain seared her heart, burning the image of James Hurley in its depths. Hers was a lost love. Twice, she had been scorned, first by Ralph and then by James, but only once had she truly loved. She loved James and always would.

"Eliza, please say you'll go with me tonight." Trennen shook her gently, bringing her eyes to focus again on his face.

"Promise you'll leave me alone after tonight?"

His head drooped, but he nodded. "If that's what you want."

She shrugged. "All right. I'll tell my father."

Eliza's mood darkened like the clouds above when she climbed into the Wingates' buggy and sank into its plush cushions. Vanda squeezed her hand while Trennen settled into the front seat beside her.

"I'm glad you came tonight." Vanda smiled, oblivious to Eliza's unhappiness. "The play is coming along well, don't you think?"

Eliza nodded.

Vanda said, "I feel so unworthy playing the part of Mary. Can you imagine what it must have been like for her? She was just a young girl, but she became the mother of our Lord. Oh, how wonderful it would be to be used of God."

"You'd better not let Pop hear you talking that way." Trennen spoke across Eliza.

Vanda looked down at her hands. "I know. I keep praying for him, but. . .sometimes I get discouraged. I'm so afraid something will happen to him, and he won't know Jesus."

Trennen laughed. "You should worry about what happens to you if he finds out you're still coming here."

Vanda sighed. "I suppose." She was quiet as they dropped off three small children.

Eliza was glad the next stop would be hers, as she wanted desperately to close herself in her bedroom, climb in her bed, and have a good cry in her pillow.

But Trennen turned the horses south, away from her father's house. She looked at him in alarm. "Where are you going?"

He laughed. "Relax, Eliza. I have to take Vanda and Cletis home and then turn around and come back into town, anyway. You don't really mind, do you?"

Eliza did mind, but when she looked at Trennen's lazy grin and saw the determined light in his eyes, she knew it would do no good to protest. She shook her head and settled back.

They turned down the same road she had taken two months earlier with James. When the barn and the toolshed came into view, she remembered the kiss she had shared with James.

She turned her face away from the house as they drove past. James was in town, working with her father on a rush order, but she didn't want to be reminded of the wonderful day she had spent there.

Less than a mile farther down the road Trennen turned the buggy into a yard cluttered with various wagon parts and tools.

Vanda stiffened. "Poppa's home."

Cletis spoke from the backseat in a small voice. "Take us back to town with you, Trennen."

"Naw." He stepped down. "You wouldn't have anyplace to stay. Come on. I'll go in and talk to him."

Vanda lifted her chin as Trennen came around the buggy to help her down. "No, Trennen. You take Eliza home. We'll be fine."

"Vanda, why don't you come back to town?" Eliza caught her friend's hand as she climbed down. "You could stay with me. Lenny would love to have Cletis come."

Vanda shook her head. She gave Eliza a smile. "Thank you, but we can't. Someone has to take care of Poppa." She jumped to the ground. "Don't worry. We'll be fine."

As Cletis crawled from the buggy, Vanda turned to Trennen. "You go on and take Eliza home. It wouldn't do for Poppa to see you right now. You know he doesn't like you working for the Wingates. It'd just make things worse."

As Trennen guided the buggy back out onto the road and turned it toward town, Eliza looked over her shoulder to see the door close behind Vanda. "Are you sure she'll be all right?"

"Why wouldn't she be?" Trennen shrugged. "He probably won't lay a hand on her."

He turned and looked down at Eliza's worried expression. "Aw, don't worry about Vanda. What would your father do if you did something he didn't want you to?"

She spoke quietly. "When I was little, he spanked me. Mostly, he talks to me." She smiled. "I think the talks hurt the most."

His arm encircled her, drawing her close to his side. "Sit over here where it's warmer."

They were nearing the Hurley house. Eliza shrank against Trennen's side, turning her face away from the house.

He hugged her even closer, his hand rubbing her upper arm. His head lowered toward hers. They were in front of James's house. She turned away. "Trennen, we're in front of a house."

"You know who lives there, too, don't you?" His voice sounded angry.

She nodded. "But that doesn't—"

"Oh, it matters all right. I know all about you and Hurley. I've seen the way you look at him."

They were past the house now. Trennen's mouth covered hers in a rough kiss that frightened her. She pulled away. He let go of the reins, giving the horses their heads. They slowed to a leisurely stroll. "You are mine, Eliza. No one else is going to have you." He held her with both hands, his kisses now forceful and demanding.

She struggled for freedom. His voice sounded hoarse, his breathing ragged. "Don't fight me, Eliza. I love you."

She fought with everything she had. She screamed, but there was no one to hear. She beat at him, trying to push him back. He pinned her against the cushion. She kicked at him. He cursed.

The horses became skittish as the buggy bounced with their struggles.

Her head felt light and dizzy. She had to get away before she fainted. But Trennen pushed her into the corner of the seat. Fear rose within her.

Then as if a voice spoke within her head, she heard the words, *"Call upon Me in the day of trouble: I will deliver thee, and thou shalt glorify Me."*

"Lord Jesus, help me." Her cry came from the depths of her heart, and she knew her Lord would hear.

In the next instant she saw the buggy whip. She stopped struggling as her hand closed around it. She cracked the whip over the horses' backs, startling them. They reared and came down in a run, whinnying with fright.

Trennen fell off balance, landing on the floor with a cry of pain. Cool air rushed in where Trennen had been, and Eliza knew she was free. She scrambled to the side and, without thinking of the consequences, jumped from the racing buggy.

⁂

James stood outside on the street while Orval closed and locked the door of the cooperage.

"I sure appreciate you staying tonight," his boss said.

"That's all right. I'm glad to see it done."

The two men walked around the building to where James's horse and Orval's buggy waited.

James flexed his shoulders, then pulled his collar up around his neck before reaching for his horse's reins. A misty rain began to fall. "Think it might turn to snow before morning?"

"Could be," Orval said. "My girls always thought we should have snow for Christmas. Maybe they'll get their wish this year." He climbed into his buggy. "Take care going home. If this picks up before you get there, you'll be soaked."

James swung into the saddle and nodded. "I'll see you in the morning at church."

He rode at a brisk trot, glad that the cold mist fell against his back. He'd soon be home in the dry with a cup of hot coffee in his hands. His mind turned to the subject that had haunted him day and night for two months. What had he done to Eliza?

He shouldn't have taken the liberty of kissing her behind the toolshed, but she hadn't seemed to mind at the time. His heart quickened at the memory.

He'd tried time after time to talk to her, but she always cut him off. He frowned as he thought of Trennen. What did Eliza think she was doing, walking out with a fellow like that?

As he turned down the road to his house, he saw buggy lanterns coming toward him. It seemed odd that someone would be out so late on such a miserable night. The buggy came fast and then veered toward him as if trying to run him off the road.

James pulled his horse to the side, narrowly missing a collision. As it whipped past, he recognized the Wingate buggy. He was almost certain Trennen sat bent over in the driver's seat. He must be in an awfully big hurry.

James went on, hunching his shoulders against the rain while he watched for any more surprises. Then several yards before he reached his house, he heard a soft moan from the side of the road. He reined in and dismounted.

🙟

Eliza lay in a crumpled heap. She heard the buggy go on without her and then a blackness, darker than night, closed in, taking her away from the terror she had just experienced.

"Eliza, what are you doing here? Are you hurt?" Gentle hands scooped her up, and she moaned in answer to the distant voice.

She tried to open her eyes, but her lids were so heavy. She laid her head on the man's shoulder, trying to burrow deeper into his arms.

He groaned. "Oh, Eliza, my love. If he's hurt you, as God is my witness, I'll make him pay."

She tried to respond, to tell him she wasn't hurt, but she was so sleepy. She couldn't keep her eyes open, and the words wouldn't come.

Then they were at his house.

❧

James struggled with the door, and his sister opened it. She looked at his burden with wide eyes. "What happened? What are you doing with. . . ?"

"I found her by the side of the road just outside," James interrupted as he brushed past. "Mother, can I put her on your bed?"

"Of course." She led the way and then pulled the covers back as James carefully lay Eliza down. He knelt by the bed to unlace Eliza's shoes and slip them from her feet. He pulled the covers up, pausing when he saw her torn dress. His gaze moved to her face where a new bruise marred one pale cheek just under her closed eyelashes. His eyes darkened and his jaw clenched as he gently tucked the covers under her chin.

"What happened, Son?"

He turned toward his mother and shook his head. "I'm not sure. I'm going back into town for her father and the doctor."

"I'll take care of her." Mrs. Hurley followed him back into the kitchen. "There's hot coffee on the stove. Won't you have a cup before you go back out?"

"I can't take the time. If anything happens to her. . ." He didn't finish, but he knew his mother understood.

James couldn't push his horse fast enough. The mist had

turned to a gentle drizzle, and it hit him full in the face, but he hardly noticed. All he could think of was the girl in his mother's bed. Would she be all right? He prayed every step of the way that she would.

Lights blazed from the front of the Jacksons' house. The door opened immediately on James's knock. Mr. Jackson stood framed in the doorway. "James, have you seen Eliza?" Worry lines etched around his eyes.

"Yes, she's at my house."

"Thank God. I was just getting ready to go look for her." Orval visibly relaxed.

"Sir, something's happened to her. I think you'd better come."

Orval's face went pale. "What do you mean? Is she hurt?"

"Right now she's asleep. I'd like to get the doctor to take a look at her, if you don't mind."

"I'm going with you, Orval." Mary crowded close to her husband's side.

"It's raining, Mary."

"Orval, she's my daughter, too. I'll get my heavy cloak." She turned back into the house.

"May I go after the doctor, Sir?" James asked. He wanted to be on his way.

"I'd appreciate that, James." Orval nodded. "We'll be there as soon as we can."

When James reined his horse back into his own yard, the Jacksons had just arrived. He called to them before going to the barn. "Doc's on his way. Go on in."

James took care of his horse before he walked to the house. He stopped outside and looked in the direction of town. Right now Eliza was his primary concern, but tomorrow would find him at Trennen Von Hall's door.

She was still asleep. Mary sat beside the bed, holding her hand. Orval sat by his wife, his eyes never leaving his daughter's face.

The doctor came in a bustle of reassurance. He shooed all

but Mary from the room. James paced the kitchen floor, finally throwing himself into a chair at the table when his mother pushed a cup of coffee into his hands.

He watched the closed door, willing it to open. How he longed for Eliza to look up at him again with her saucy little grin. He hadn't known how much he could miss her sharp tongue until now.

"James, I'm sure she'll be all right." His mother rested her hand on his shoulder.

"Trennen did this to her." He still watched the door.

Orval turned at his words. "I figured as much. He was supposed to bring her home. He must have decided to take his brother and sister home first."

"So he could get her alone." The words stuck in James's throat. "But he won't get away with it."

"There's the doctor now." Mrs. Hurley's hand tightened on James's shoulder as the door opened.

James tried to see past the doctor, but he pulled the door closed and crossed the room to the woodstove. He held his hands above it, warming them. "Before you go in, Mr. Jackson, I've a few words to say. She's awake now, but she's upset."

James's heart skipped a beat.

"The young man she was with suffered a broken arm when the horses got away from him. I set it just before James came to get me, although at the time I didn't know there was another casualty."

"Is she hurt in any way?" Orval asked.

The doctor shook his head. "Just a few bruises. She'll be fine. You take her home tonight and put her in her own bed. Let her take it easy a couple of days, and she'll be good as new."

Orval disappeared into the bedroom and closed the door behind him. As James sat there waiting, he knew without doubt that he loved Eliza Jackson. He determined that when she was well, if she would let him within shouting distance, he would tell her just how he felt about her.

fourteen

Eliza woke to a gentle kiss on her cheek. Mary straightened and smiled at her. "How are you feeling this morning?"

"All right." Eliza turned her face toward the wall. "Where's my father?"

Mary sat on the edge of the bed. "He's gone to church.

"Eliza. . ." Mary touched her shoulder. "Can you tell me what happened last night?"

Eliza pulled the covers close. "I have a headache. I'd like to sleep."

"All right, Dear." Mary stood. "But you're going to have to face this sooner or later. Your father plans to visit with Trennen today. If he hurt you. . ."

"No." Eliza shook her head and then winced with the pain. Tears sprang to her eyes. She blotted them with the covers, keeping her face from Mary. "I jumped from the buggy."

Mary reached out and smoothed Eliza's hair. "We have a lot to thank God for."

Eliza tried to sleep, but she kept remembering. She knew Mary was right. It had taken a miracle for her to get away from Trennen and another to keep her from serious injury when she jumped.

She prayed, thanking God for His love and help. Although she felt better, heaviness remained in her heart—deadness to her soul that she didn't know what to do about. She prayed again, asking God to remove the heaviness, but still it remained. Something was keeping her from full favor with God.

At noon Father came into her room. He sat on the edge of her bed. "How are you feeling, Eliza?"

"I have a headache."

"I need to know what happened to you last night."

"What difference does it make?"

"It makes a lot of difference." Father frowned. "According to Mr. Wingate, Trennen didn't come home last night."

"He took the Wingates' buggy?"

"No, it's there, but Trennen is gone. Mr. Wingate is on his way to the Von Hall home." He shook his head. "I don't think he'd go far. According to the doctor, his arm was broken last night."

The hint of a smile broke Father's serious look. "What'd you do to him?"

Eliza looked at her father. "I prayed. Then I saw the buggy whip and cracked it across the horses. Trennen lost his balance and fell to the floor. That was when I jumped."

"And you got this bruise on your face." He tenderly touched the bruise with the back of his fingers.

Mary knocked on the door and entered, carrying a tray of food. Father stepped out of her way as she placed it across Eliza's lap. He grinned down at Eliza pushing herself upright. "So we're feeding this girl in bed, are we?"

"Don't bother Eliza." Mary straightened and playfully shoved her husband toward the door. "Your dinner's waiting downstairs."

Eliza watched them leave. She hadn't told him what Trennen had tried to do to her, but she thought her father knew, anyway.

What would Father do to Trennen? He said he planned to talk to him. At the moment she didn't care what happened to him as long as he never touched her again.

❧

James went home from church with a heavy heart. He'd hoped to confront Trennen, but it seemed the scoundrel had disappeared. He ate dinner, then went outside to care for his animals. A light snow had fallen in the early morning hours. He'd have to fork some hay down and check on his stock.

On the way to the barn, he saw the Wingate buggy drive past. His heart quickened until he realized Mr. Wingate drove it. He waved and went on to the barn.

He'd just finished with the hay when he heard his name called. "James. James, I need your help."

Mr. Wingate hurried toward the barn as James ran out. "It's Vanda. She's been hurt bad. Come, help me." His sentences came out in gasps.

James told his mother where he was going before jumping into the buggy beside Mr. Wingate.

Vanda lay on a small cot in the front room of the cabin, her face a stark contrast to her dark hair spread out on the pillow. A thin blanket covered her, and the room felt like ice. Her face, with one eye swollen shut, was bruised almost beyond recognition. She appeared to be sleeping.

James looked at Mr. Wingate's ashen face. "Where's Cletis?"

"I don't know. He's not here."

James reached out and touched Vanda's neck. A faint pulse beat under his fingers. "She's still alive, but she won't be if we don't get help."

Vanda moaned as he picked her up, blanket and all. He tried to carry her as gently as he could. He laid her on the back seat of the buggy, then climbed in and put her head on his lap. He tried to cushion her as best he could to help smooth the ride.

James breathed a prayer of thanks when Mr. Wingate stopped in front of the doctor's house. They hurriedly carried Vanda into the doctor's examining room. As the doctor probed for broken bones and internal injuries, Mr. Wingate's plump face turned red with indignation. "It's that no-good father of hers, I'll wager. We tried to help the children, but he wouldn't hear of it."

The doctor nodded. "I know you did what you could. No one in this town can fault you there."

James felt cheated when the blame shifted from Trennen, but he shrugged off his personal feelings and asked the doctor,

"Will she be all right?"

"There are some broken ribs, and as you can see, she's badly bruised." He shook his head. "Whoever did this to her did a thorough job."

"That no-good—" Mr. Wingate started.

"Yes, I've no doubt you're right about that." The doctor nodded. "But it may be tomorrow before she's able to tell us for sure."

James saw Vanda's eyelid flutter. He took a step forward. "She's coming to."

The three men crowded near. Mr. Wingate got down on one knee near her head. "Vanda, honey, who did this to you?"

Her good eye stared at him, but there was no answer. He tried again. "Did your father hit you?"

A tear ran out of her eye.

Mr. Wingate looked up. "There's your answer."

He turned back to her. "What happened to Cletis? Do you know if he took him?"

"Now you've gone and done it." The doctor frowned at Mr. Wingate. "If she didn't know he was gone, you've given her something to worry about."

"Look." James watched the slow up and down movement of her head. "She knows."

Mr. Wingate insisted that Vanda be moved to his house. After the doctor bandaged her and gave her some laudanum for pain, James carried her to the buggy and then into the Wingate home.

❧

Monday at noon, Eliza sat by her window to watch for her father. When she saw him, she pulled her dressing gown on and ran from her room. By the time she got to the kitchen door, she could hear Mary and Father talking. He said, "I suppose she's better than yesterday, but she's still in pitiful shape."

Eliza stopped, her hand on the door. She pressed close to listen.

"The poor girl." Mary sighed. "I can't understand how a father could do such a thing. Has she been able to talk yet?"

"As a matter of fact she has." A chair scraped across the floor.

Eliza pushed the door open a crack until she could see her father sitting by the table. Mary placed a buttered hot roll in front of him.

"M-m-m." He grinned his appreciation. "You're spoiling me."

Mary smiled before moving out of Eliza's sight. "What about Vanda being able to talk?"

Vanda had been hurt. Why hadn't they told her? Eliza pushed the door open and stormed into the room. "What's wrong with Vanda?"

"Should you be out of bed?" Father rushed to her side, taking her arm.

She jerked away. "I'm not sick. I want to know about Vanda. What's happened to her?"

Father told what he knew and that Vanda was now at the Wingates'.

"Father, I want to see her."

"I don't think so." He shook his head.

"Please, Father."

"Would it hurt for her to go just for a few minutes?" Mary intervened on Eliza's behalf.

He frowned. "She's been beaten, Eliza, almost to death. You won't recognize her."

Although Father argued, in the end, Eliza won.

She dressed with care in a blue dress made with thin balloon oversleeves. She selected the matching blue bonnet that looked like a hat with a wide rim framing her head. She tied the blue satin ribbons in a wide bow. She wanted to look her best for Vanda.

Yet when she saw her, she realized her father had been right. The purple, swollen face that turned toward her was unrecognizable.

"It's me, Eliza." The voice sounded like Vanda's, although

slurred. "Sit here by me."

Eliza wiped tears away as she sat on the bed.

Vanda smiled and closed her hand around Eliza's. "It isn't as bad as it looks. I think he just hit me a couple of times in the face."

"Oh, Vanda, how can you joke about it?" Eliza wanted to cry.

"I'm not joking. I think that's what happened."

"But it looks like he ran your face through the sausage mill."

Eliza was surprised at Vanda's laugh. "Oh, that hurts." She quickly composed herself. "Here you sit, pretty as a picture, and tell me how ugly I am."

"I didn't mean that," Eliza quickly assured her and then saw the twinkle in the other girl's eye. "Oh. You're joking again. After what you've been through, I'd think you'd need to be cheered up instead of the other way around."

Vanda's eyes grew serious. "You have a bruise, too. I heard you went through a bad experience that same night."

Eliza's eyes widened. "How did you hear?"

Vanda's mouth twisted into a small, lopsided smile. "I'm learning to be quiet and listen." Her smile vanished. "At least Trennen won't bother you anymore."

Eliza's heartbeat increased. "What do you mean by that?"

"He left this morning on the stage."

Eliza frowned. "No one told me."

"They aren't telling me, either. I suppose they think I'm not strong enough." Again she smiled. "They don't know that the Lord is my strength."

Eliza smiled tenderly at her friend. "Father said the entire church is praying for your quick recovery."

"Then I will be out of this bed in time for the Christmas program." Vanda's eyes shone. "I want to see it even if I can't be Mary." Her hand moved to touch her side. "I only have a couple of broken ribs. That won't keep me down long."

"I'm sure it won't." Eliza wondered how Vanda could possibly be up and around in little more than a week.

Vanda reached out and squeezed Eliza's hand. "Do you remember I asked you to pray for my father?"

Eliza nodded.

"I'd like for you to pray with me even harder now." A tear rolled from Vanda's eye. "I don't know where he is or what he's doing, but I'm afraid he will die without knowing Jesus."

"Aren't you angry with him for what he did? You almost died. You would have if they hadn't found you."

Vanda shook her head. "He didn't know what he was doing. Don't you see, Eliza? My sins nailed Jesus to the cross. How can I help but forgive others when I have been forgiven so much?"

Eliza sat and stared at her friend. Vanda meant what she said. Eliza bowed her head. She nodded. "I'll join you in praying for your father."

Eliza didn't stay long after that. She needed the privacy of her room where she could think and pray. Vanda was a babe in Christ, but she had taught Eliza something that she would never forget as long as she lived.

For hours Eliza stayed shut away in her room, where the others thought she was resting. Instead she fell to her knees beside her bed, alternately reading God's Word and praying. At first unwilling to give up her own feelings, she finally saw herself honestly for the first time in many months as God revealed what she would have to do in order to be brought back to the right relationship with Him that she craved.

After a time, she arose and washed away the tears of her soul-searching. She glanced out the window and saw it was still too early for her father to be home from work. She needed to talk to Mary.

Mary sat at the table peeling potatoes for supper.

Eliza sat in a chair across the table, unsure of how to begin. How could she break down the wall she had built with a simple apology? But she knew she must try.

Mary turned to smile at her. "Did you have a nice rest, Dear?"

Eliza shook her head. "I was praying about something that's been bothering me."

"Is it anything I can help with?"

Eliza smiled at Mary. "I think I already have my answer. Do you have a moment?"

"Of course."

Eliza looked into Mary's kind, green eyes. "Do you love my father? I mean, really love him?"

A tinge of pink touched Mary's cheeks. She smiled and nodded. "I love your father very much. I thank God every day that He led you to introduce us."

Eliza bowed her head as moisture clouded her vision. "I've been terrible."

Mary's hand stretched across the table to cover Eliza's with a sympathetic touch. "You've had a hard time adjusting, but God has assured us all along that you would come through this."

"You've been praying for me?"

"I pray for you every day, Eliza. I care about you. I loved you before I loved your father, you know. You were my friend, and then you were my daughter."

Eliza looked up at Mary, disbelief covering her face. Mary had forgiven her before she even asked.

But Mary misread Eliza's expression. "No, I don't mean I'm trying to take your mother's place. No one could do that, and I wouldn't want to. She will always have a special place in your heart and in your father's. That's only right. But don't you see? It's the same with me. I already have one daughter, yet I have plenty of room in my heart to love five more. That doesn't mean I love Kathrene less. It just means I love you as much."

Tears streamed down Eliza's face. All she could do was choke out the words, "I love you, too, Mary. I'm so sorry."

She didn't remember moving out of her chair, but she found herself kneeling on the floor with her head in Mary's lap.

Mary stroked her hair, crooning words of forgiveness as the healing tears fell.

Finally, Eliza pulled away, her face wet with tears, a smile on her lips. She reached out and took both of Mary's hands in hers. "I'm so glad I came to talk to you."

"I am, too." Mary smiled through her own tears. "You don't know how glad."

"What's going on here?" Neither had noticed Father come in. He stood looking from one to the other.

Eliza jumped up and grabbed him around the neck. "I love you, Father."

His arms slipped around her as he held her close. "I love you, too, Eliza." He looked over her head at Mary, his eyebrows lifted in question.

Mary stood. "Eliza and I have just come to a wonderful understanding." She stepped to her husband's side, and he put one arm around her. "We've decided there's room in our hearts for each other and for you, too."

Father let out a long breath. "That's the best news I've heard in a long time."

❧

The next day Eliza returned to visit Vanda. She went every day that week, each time noticing an improvement in Vanda's condition. Still, no word came about Cletis and his father. Eliza knew Vanda worried about them. On Friday, as Eliza left, Vanda caught her hand and held it. "Eliza, would you pray with me right now for Cletis and Poppa?"

Eliza nodded. Still holding Vanda's hand, she knelt beside the bed, and together the girls prayed that God would protect the two and bring them to salvation.

The following week when Eliza prayed with her friend again, Vanda kept her hand. "Wait, Eliza, please."

Eliza remained on her knees.

"I know what Trennen did to you. I know Uncle Charles sent him away because of it. And I wouldn't blame you if you don't want to, but I think he needs our prayers, too."

Eliza hesitated only a moment. "I'll pray with you for your brother."

As Vanda's physical strength returned, Eliza's spiritual strength grew. She spent more time in prayer and Bible reading during those weeks than she had in the past two years. Her relationship with Mary became a treasure. Kathrene, when she wasn't with Stephen, responded to Eliza's encouragement to become the sister she had always wanted to be.

But there was still one dark spot in Eliza's life. She could not forget James Hurley. Every time she thought of him, a dart driven by Lenny's words pierced her heart. *Father got you James, didn't he?* It hurt more every day.

A light snow began to fall Sunday afternoon. That evening, buggies and wagons arrived early for the Christmas program. The church shone with candles and lanterns and buzzed with the excited voices of parents and children alike. Both front corners of the church had been partitioned off with sheets and quilts to make two small rooms where the actors could get into costume. Eliza wound her way behind Lenny through the crowded church.

Someone jostled her, and she fell into James. His hands closed over her upper arms to steady her, and he did not let go. She found herself eye level with his mouth. Her gaze lifted to his dark gray eyes frowning down at her.

"Are you all right, Miss Jackson?"

At the formal use of her name, she stiffened and pulled back. "I'm just fine, thank you, Mr. Hurley. Now if you'll excuse me, I'm supposed to be an angel tonight."

A slow smile spread across his face. "That should be interesting."

"Oh!" She jerked away and moved as quickly as she could to the corner where the angels were dressing. She slipped through a space between two quilts, glad to be out of his sight. She knew her face flamed.

"Eliza, here's your costume." Kathrene tossed it to her, then slipped into her own. Eliza carefully wrapped the sheet around herself, and Kathrene tied it into place. The halo and wings were harder to keep on, but finally all three angels were ready.

"Who's going to play Mary now that Vanda isn't able to?" Barbara whispered.

"I don't know," Eliza whispered back. Yesterday afternoon at their last rehearsal, a replacement still hadn't been announced.

The program began with the small children. One gave a welcome that brought a round of applause. Then several others sang "What Child Is This?"

The angels peeked through narrow cracks between quilts. Eliza could see the front of the church where most of the activity took place.

"What's going on?" She whispered to the other angels as a hush fell over the congregation and several gasps were heard. Applause filled the church. The girls could only look at each other and wonder what was happening. Then as quickly as the applause began, it stopped.

As a hush fell on the congregation, Eliza saw a hooded Mary and Joseph cross the pulpit area. Mary turned and, with Joseph's help, sank to the floor behind the manger. It was Vanda. Her face, yellow and green with bruises and still distorted by the swelling, had never looked lovelier to Eliza. A glow seemed to emanate from her serene expression. She kept her eyelids lowered in reverence. Then she reached out and lifted a doll from the straw-filled manger and cradled it in her arms.

While the shepherds came from the opposite corner, Eliza followed Barbara to stand behind Mary and Joseph. Kathrene stepped forward and sang "Angels from the Realms of Glory."

When Eliza blended her voice with Barbara's on the chorus, she felt God's presence. She was so thankful that God had given His only Son to become the sacrifice for her sins. There was no love greater than that.

❧

James sat beside his mother and watched the Christmas program. He smiled at the small children and felt proud of his younger sister, but the one person he most wanted to see was hidden from his view in the front corner of the church. He brought to mind the snapping brown eyes that were becoming a regular visitor to his dreams. He remembered the feel of her satin cheek, the softness of her dark hair caught in his fingers.

He loved Eliza Jackson, but she wanted nothing to do with him. For the thousandth time he asked himself what he had done to turn her away.

And then she stepped from the curtains that hid her and stood behind Mary and Joseph. He had made fun of her being an angel, but as he stared at her, he knew he had never seen a more beautiful angel. Her eyes lifted above the heads of the congregation as if she looked into heaven. The yellowed bruise still covered her cheek, yet a soft smile touched her radiant face, making her appear beyond the reach of earth—and man.

The dull ache in his chest had become part of him. Because she was beyond his reach. He looked down at his clenched fists. He'd tried to talk to her, but she wouldn't listen. She went out of her way to avoid him. He had to find out what was wrong if he had to have a talk with her father to do it.

❧

Winter came with a vengeance after the Christmas program. One snowfall followed another until the drifts measured more than four feet deep. Father said Old Man Winter was making up for last year's mild weather.

Eliza was glad the weather kept her from seeing James. Maybe if she didn't see him, she could forget him. She spent most of her time in the house helping Mary and Kathrene or playing with Nora. She began to look forward to spring when she would have a new brother or sister.

Then, winter gave way to spring flowers and sunshine. A time of new growth. Kathrene accepted Stephen's marriage proposal, but Eliza's life seemed to stall as her heart refused to forget James. All winter she had tried to block him from her thoughts, yet the first day she went back to church, he was there. When their eyes met, she knew she would have to learn to live with the pain of her love for him.

One day Father came home from work at noon with some news. He came into the kitchen where the women were working, a large smile on his face. "You'll never guess who just arrived in town."

Lenny came into the kitchen from the parlor. Father reached out and ruffled his hair. "You'll be wanting to hear this, too."

"Tell us who before we burst with curiosity," Mary said.

"Cletis Von Hall."

"Cletis!" Eliza squealed before Lenny could react. "Was his father with him? Where had he been? Did he go see Vanda? Oh, she'll be so happy he's all right. Is he, Father?"

Father laughed. "Yes, Eliza, Cletis is fine. As soon as we told him where Vanda was, he went to see her." Then he grew serious. "His father wasn't with him."

Silence fell around the table as her father related the story told to him. "After Von Hall beat Vanda unconscious, he picked her up and put her on the cot in the main room of the cabin. He covered her with a blanket, but when she remained limp and unresponsive, he thought she was dead.

"Cletis said his father panicked and ran, taking him. By the time they got to a town called Rolla, Mr. Von Hall was desperate for more whiskey, but he didn't have the money. He shook like he had a chill, and then he broke down and cried. He was like that for hours until he slept. When he woke, he took Cletis into town. They stopped at the first church they came to. Cletis said he didn't know what happened there except his father talked to the preacher, and he wasn't shaking anymore. The preacher went with them to the sheriff."

"He turned himself in." Eliza frowned. "Why didn't we hear anything? Wouldn't they have checked to see if Vanda really died?"

"Yes, except before they could, the weather got bad. A fire broke out in a house next to the jail. The two prisoners were released to help fight it. Von Hall heard a little girl crying. He perished saving her life."

Eliza scarcely noticed the tears running down her face. God had granted Vanda's wish to be used by Him.

"Cletis stayed with the minister until the weather cleared enough to send him home."

❧

The next morning, Eliza put on her nicest visiting dress and went with Lenny to the Wingates' house. Mrs. Wingate took Lenny back to the kitchen to eat a snack with Cletis, leaving the two girls alone in the parlor. They met in the middle of the room and hugged. Eliza couldn't stop the tears.

As they pulled apart, she said, "I'm sorry, Vanda, about what's happened."

Vanda nodded. "Thank you. God knows what's best for us. I'll always remember my father died a hero. And I have Cletis back."

"Yes, how is he?"

Vanda smiled. "I don't think you'd recognize him. Oh, he looks about the same, but he doesn't act it. He was so rebellious before, but now he's trying really hard to do right. He even asked me if I thought God loved him."

"That's wonderful, Vanda."

"Yes, and that's not all." Vanda sat on the edge of a chair. Her eyes shone. "Cletis and I are going away. We have an aunt in Boston who wants us to come live with her. She has no children. Uncle Charles says she and her husband are a wonderful Christian couple who will probably spoil us rotten."

"Oh, Vanda!" Eliza couldn't help the cry of dismay that leapt to her lips. "You can't leave."

"I know, Eliza." Vanda crossed to the sofa and sat beside

her, putting her arm around her shoulders. "I'll miss you, but I believe this is for the best. I want Cletis to grow up in a home where there is discipline and love. I think he will have that with our aunt and uncle."

"Why couldn't he get that here?"

"Uncle Charles and Aunt Martha do love us, but they are too close to all that's happened. And they aren't as young as our other aunt and uncle." Vanda smiled. "Besides, I have a feeling Cletis will need a father young enough to keep up with him."

Eliza knew in her heart that Vanda was right, yet she knew she would never forget her friend.

fifteen

Vanda left the first week of April. Eliza stood by the stagecoach with her. Vanda wore a soft blue dress of the latest fashion, and Eliza knew several more new dresses were packed in her trunk. Mrs. Wingate had made sure her niece and nephew would not be ashamed when they arrived at their new home. Eliza waited while the others told Vanda goodbye, and then she stepped forward.

"I don't know how I'll ever get along without you." She hugged Vanda with tears in her eyes.

"You promised to not cry." Vanda hugged Eliza tight. "I'll write to you as soon as I get there."

"You'd better." Eliza forced a smile. "Because I can't write to you until I get your address, and as soon as you're gone, I'll think of a million things to tell you."

"Eliza, you're the best friend I've ever had. If it hadn't been for you, I'd never have found Jesus as my Lord."

"I didn't do anything."

"Oh, yes, you did. At first I only went to church because you were there. You were my friend, and I wanted to be with you. Then the message of God's salvation got through to me, and I went because I knew there was something missing in my life. If you hadn't been my friend, I'd have never heard that message."

Eliza could only say, "I'm glad."

"You're not going to leave without telling me good-bye, are you?" James's voice called from behind Eliza. Her heart began the hard quick pound that had become all too familiar in his presence.

"Of course not." Vanda extended her hand, and James shook it.

"This town will miss you two very much, you know." James smiled down at Vanda.

"Oh, I don't know about that." Vanda returned his smile. "But I do know we'll miss all of you."

"You take care." James turned as if to leave.

"I will." A twinkle entered Vanda's eyes. "And you take care of my friend."

James looked at Eliza. His eyes were serious as he said, "There's nothing I would like better." Then he turned and walked away.

"Better get aboard, Miss," the driver called from the open door of the coach.

"I've got to go." Vanda gave Eliza another hug. She whispered near her ear, "Be good to James." Then she and Cletis climbed on the stage.

Eliza stood by the side of the road, waving until Vanda disappeared in a cloud of dust.

&

The next day, Kathrene came in from an outing with Stephen. Her eyes shone. "Eliza, do you want to hear something funny?"

Eliza sank into a nearby chair. "It would probably be more entertaining than what I've been doing."

Kathrene sat on the sofa. "Stephen has been keeping things from me, but today he confessed."

Eliza sat a little straighter.

"We went out to look at the house." Kathrene clasped her hands in front. "Eliza, he's building a mansion for me."

Eliza frowned. She was sure Kathrene would think anything Stephen built was perfect. But really! How could a penniless beggar. . . ?

"Remember how we all thought he was poor?"

Eliza nodded.

"He isn't poor at all." Kathrene laughed. "He just wanted me to think that because he wanted me to love him for himself and not for his money."

"What would make him do that?" Eliza was as puzzled by Stephen as she had been the first time she'd seen him.

Kathrene sobered. "He's from New York where his father owns some factories and several other businesses. His father wanted him, along with his younger brother, to take over the businesses." She paused. "Stephen was engaged to be married before."

Eliza's eyes widened. "What happened?"

"He found out she was marrying him for his money. He was deeply hurt and angry. So he sold his share of the businesses to his brother, reinvested a lot of it in some regional railroads, and came west."

"But Kathrene, what if he wants to return to New York someday? Would you go with him?"

Kathrene shook her head. "I don't think I have to worry about that. Stephen has assured me that Missouri is where he wants to live and die. He knows I'm not marrying him for what he can give me. And he knows the people here like and respect him for himself, not because of his money."

She held up her hand. "Please, Eliza, don't ever tell anyone just how wealthy Stephen is. He loves it here, and he wants to make a home for us where we can be like our neighbors."

"Are you telling me that Stephen is even more wealthy than the Wingates?" Eliza could scarcely believe that.

Kathrene laughed. "I'm afraid so, but you'd never know it, would you?"

"What about your house? Is it really a mansion?"

"I might have exaggerated on that. It's a very nice two-story frame house." Kathrene smiled. "Eliza, I really love Stephen. I'd be content to live in a log cabin at the edge of town as long as I can be with him. I don't care about his money."

 largeinteger

One morning in mid-April, about an hour before Father was due home for dinner, Mary called to Eliza, "Would you please run and get your father? Tell him I'm not feeling well."

As Eliza started to go, Mary called to her again, "If you see Kathrene, please tell her to come to my bedroom."

Eliza ran up the stairs as fast as she could and pounded on Kathrene's bedroom door before jerking it open. "Kathrene, your mother needs you right away in her bedroom. I think it's her time."

Eliza left the house in a run until she reached the business part of town.

With her breath coming in gasps, she passed the cooperage and stuck her head in the chandler shop. The front room was empty. She crossed to the back room. No one was there, either. As she turned around and started back across the showroom, James opened the door and came inside.

They stood for an eternity staring at each other. He spoke first. "I thought you were a customer."

How could she speak past her pounding heart? "It's Mary. Where's my father?"

Immediately he understood the problem. "He left just a minute ago to make a delivery. I'll catch him." He stopped at the door. "Do you want to wait here?"

She followed him as he went around the building where his horse stood grazing. She watched him saddle the horse, trying to decide what she should do. Kathrene was with Mary. Surely they wouldn't need her. Maybe she should stay and watch the shops until either Father or James returned.

"What about the doctor? Do you want me to leave word with him, too?" James swung into the saddle.

At her nod, he smiled. "Don't worry. I'll give your father my horse; then I'll make the delivery and come right back." He nudged his horse forward, calling over his shoulder. "If you decide to leave, be sure and put the closed signs in the doors."

She watched him spur his horse into a run before she turned back toward the chandler shop. She opened the door, stepped inside, and collapsed onto the stool behind Father's high counter. Her knees and hands trembled. She crossed her arms on the counter and laid her head on them, trying to still the tremors that passed through her body. She prayed for Mary, asking God to give her a safe delivery and a healthy child.

"Are you all right, Eliza?" Mrs. Johnson stood in the middle of the shop, a concerned expression on her face.

Eliza smiled at the elderly lady. "Yes, I'm fine. Is there anything I can help you with?"

By the time Mrs. Johnson had made her selections and gone, Eliza figured James had caught up to Father. Maybe he was on his way home. And that was exactly where she should be going. If she waited around the shops, James would come back, and she'd be alone with him. She didn't want to take that chance.

But before Eliza could close the shops, Mr. Morrison stopped with an order for barrels. He finally left, and she put the closed sign in the shop window. As she turned to leave, James pulled Father's wagon in and stopped. As usual her heart pounded when she saw him.

James jumped from the wagon and moved to her side. "I'm glad you're still here. I was afraid you'd go home."

He stood too close. "I'd really like to talk to you, Eliza."

"Whatever would we have to talk about?" She stepped back from his overpowering height. If she didn't get away, she might cave in and cry.

"Your father seems to think you're unhappy." He got no further.

Her head snapped up. She glared at him. "How dare you and my father discuss me! I am not your concern."

She pushed past him, then stopped long enough to fling one last remark at him, "I am also not a charity case, and I'll thank you to remember that."

❧

James watched Eliza disappear around the corner. What had she meant by her being a charity case? He shook his head. There was no understanding a woman when she was riled.

But what had he done to make Eliza so angry with him?

He glanced at the wagon and smiled. Maybe there was one way to insure she stayed put long enough to find out what had got her back up. He'd have to wait a few days until the Jackson family settled down, but at the first opportunity, he'd enlist Mr. Jackson's help.

❧

The entire family crowded around the bed where Mary lay propped up, her face beaming with pride as she looked at Father. He sat on the side of the bed, a small bundle of blankets in his arms.

"Eliza, come see our new sister." Kathrene took her arm and pulled her to Father's side. "We've all been promised a chance to hold her, but Father's being a hog."

"You'll get your turn." Father looked up with a grin. He pulled a tiny hand from the blanket.

Nora squealed as the miniature fingers curled around Father's big one. "I hold my lovey."

She jumped on Mary's knees, and Father laughed. "Whoa, Girl. You'll be hurting Mama doing that."

Immediately Nora stopped. "I sorry, Mama." She plopped down beside her father, her little legs stretched out. "I want my lovey."

"All right." Father passed the baby to Nora, keeping his hands under her head and back. "We'll start with the youngest and work our way back up to me."

"Be careful, Orval." Mary tried to see. "Don't let her drop her."

"Don't worry. I've got a good hold."

While Nora and Lenny got their turns with the baby, Eliza stepped to Mary's side. "Are you all right?" She clasped Mary's hand in both of hers.

Mary smiled. "I'm fine."

"Kathrene and I can take care of everything." Eliza remembered how tired her mother had been after Nora's birth. She had never regained her strength. She didn't want the same thing to happen to Mary.

Mary smiled and reached for Kathrene's hand with her other hand. "You don't know how much I appreciate both of you."

Eliza took her turn at holding the baby. The small bundle felt so light in her arms. She pulled the blanket back to see a tiny face framed by light brown hair with a hint of red in it. The little rosebud lips made a sucking motion and then grew quiet. The baby's eyes that had been closed in sleep opened and seemed to study her big sister's face. Love, as great as she had ever felt for Nora, swept through Eliza's heart. This baby was her sister.

She looked up at her father. "I wish Cora and Vickie and Ben could see her."

He nodded. "I know. I do, too."

"She's so perfect." Eliza was totally captivated. "What is her name?"

Kathrene reached for the baby. "Why don't you discuss a name with our parents while I hold my little sister?"

Eliza placed a kiss on the tiny forehead before relinquishing the baby to Kathrene. "Be careful with her."

"Eliza, I know how to hold a baby."

Father turned to Mary. "Have you picked a name?"

Mary shook her head. "Nothing I've thought of sounds right."

Eliza lifted Nora and sat with her on the bed. "How about you, Nora? Do you have any good ideas? What do you want us to call the baby?"

"Her's my lovey," Nora said.

Eliza squeezed her little sister. "Yes, she's a sweet little lovey just like you, but I don't think we want to name her that."

"Lovey, Lovelle, Lovena." Mary tried changing the word slightly. "Why can't we make our own name with some variation of that? I like the idea. It could mean sweet little loved one."

Father looked thoughtful. "What's wrong with Lovena?"

"Or we could spell it with a *u* so it's more like a name. How about Luvena?" Eliza suggested. "What about Luvena Anne or Luvena Marie?"

"Luvena Marie Jackson," Mary repeated and smiled. "I like it. What do you think, Orval?"

He nodded. "It sounds like our littlest girl has a name."

❧

Luvena, or Lovey, as Nora insisted on calling her, was a quiet baby. She slept most of the day, crying only when she had need of attention. And attention was one thing she had no lack of.

One day as Eliza rocked her little sister to sleep, she noticed Mary in the doorway of her bedroom watching them. A smile played around the corners of her mouth. "You are going to have that baby so spoiled no one can do anything with her."

"You don't really think love will spoil her, do you?" Eliza asked.

Mary reached down and took her baby. "No, and neither will rocking."

She stopped at the door, turning to say, "I'm going to put Luvena in her own bed, and then you and I are going to get your father's meal."

At dinner, Father looked across the table at Eliza. "How long has it been since you helped me with the shops?"

"Not counting the day Luvena was born?" At his nod, she thought back and couldn't remember the last time. She shrugged her shoulders. "I don't know. A long time, I guess."

He seemed interested in his food. "I've got a delivery needs to be made this afternoon. How'd you like to go along?"

"I'll go with you, Father." Lenny stopped chewing long enough to volunteer.

"No, this time I want Eliza to go. I'll tell you what, Lenny; you can go on the next delivery I have to make. How's that?" At Lenny's nod, Father looked back at Eliza. "How about it? There's a blue sky above and April flowers coming up all over the place. You couldn't pick a prettier day to go for a ride in the country."

She laughed. "All right. As soon as the dishes are done, I'll come."

"Eliza, I can do the dishes. Why don't you go on with Father now?" Kathrene urged her.

"Will we leave on the delivery right away?" Eliza didn't want to chance another encounter with James.

"Sure. The wagon's already loaded and sitting in back of the shops."

"All right, then." Eliza nodded. "I'll go." She knew Father had been concerned about her. If it'd make him feel better, she'd go with him. Besides, it was a beautiful day.

Her steps lagged as they approached her father's shops. Above all, she did not want to see James. She edged toward the side of the building. "I'll go around back and wait in the wagon."

Father nodded. "That's fine. I need to go inside for a moment." He waved her on as they parted. "This won't take long."

James was nowhere in sight. Eliza sighed with relief and climbed on the wagon. A bird scolded her from the branches of a nearby tree. She adjusted her skirts and tried to find the bird. The dense covering of green leaves hid it well. She tilted her head back and looked all the way to the top of the tree. The scolding went on, and still she couldn't see it. Slowly, her eyes searched for the bird, branch by branch. She became so engrossed in finding the bird she didn't realize her father had returned until she felt the wagon move as he climbed on.

A flicker of blue in the tree caught her attention then, and without turning to look at him, she pointed at it. "Look up there, Father. Do you see that bird? He's been making a racket ever since he saw me, but I've just now found him."

When Father didn't answer but flicked the reins over the horse instead, Eliza turned to see what was wrong.

James looked back at her.

"No," the cry tore from her throat. "I will not go with you. Where is my father?"

The wagon moved forward. James shrugged. "Your father's in the shop, and you are going with me."

"James, I assure you, if you do not stop this wagon now and let me off, I'll jump."

With the speed of lightning, James grabbed her arm and pulled her close to his side. "You're just the little spitfire who would do that, aren't you?"

They pulled out and turned north down the Booneville Road. James's arm slipped around her shoulders. "James, let go of me." Eliza spoke through clenched teeth. Her heart pounded hard in her chest. "This is not proper. People are looking at us."

He grinned at her. "If you promise to behave yourself, I'll let go."

She tried to sit as dignified as possible with her side pressed against James. "All right. Let me go, and I won't jump." At his triumphant look, she added, "I won't talk to you, either."

They were past the business part of town, where the houses spread out thin. James relaxed his hold on her, letting her scoot as far as she could get from him. He nodded. "I guess that's a pretty good bargain. With your mouth shut, I might be able to tell you a thing or two."

She turned to him with fire in her eyes. "Like how much my father's paying you for this little excursion."

He looked at her with a puzzled expression "He doesn't pay me extra for deliveries. Besides, what's that got to do with anything?"

"It has everything to do with it, and you know it." She retreated back into silence.

James shook his head. "If you're ready to not talk now, I'd like to talk to you."

"I told you I wouldn't talk to you, didn't I?" She refused to look at him.

"Yes, but it doesn't sound like you're ready."

"I'm ready anytime. But I'll have to warn you. I don't plan to listen to anything you have to say."

James let a burst of air escape through his teeth. "Eliza, you are the most aggravating woman I have ever met." After a second, he added. "You're also the prettiest."

She swung around to look at him, but he stared ahead down the road. "In the last six months, I don't know how many times I've tried to talk to you. But every time I start to say something, you run away or do something to stop me."

"I don't see any reason for us to talk."

"Well, I do." James raised his voice as he turned to look into her eyes. "Were you in love with Trennen?"

Eliza gasped. How could he ask her such a stupid question? She glared at him and then shifted in her seat.

"Eliza! You either sit still, or you sit over here where I can keep hold of you." At his commanding tone she froze.

A smile curved her lips. "I wasn't going to jump, James."

"Then answer my question. Were you, or are you, in love with Trennen?"

"That's ridiculous." She looked out at the countryside they were passing through. "In the first place it's none of your business, and in the second place it's insulting to know that anyone would even think I possibly could be."

James let his breath out in a *whish*. Eliza looked at him and saw a wide grin on his face. For some reason his happiness just added fuel to her anger.

"For your information, James Hurley, I think Trennen Von Hall is an extremely handsome man." She felt victory as his grin disappeared. But she couldn't help adding, "At first I enjoyed his company, but it didn't take long for that to wear thin."

"Then why did you continue keeping company with him?"

"Because I couldn't get rid of him. I told him I didn't want to see him anymore, but he wouldn't listen. I was scared of him. I didn't know what to do."

"Why didn't you tell your father?" James's jaw clenched. He hadn't known the extent of Eliza's problems with Trennen.

"I didn't think of it," Eliza answered his question. "I kept thinking he would leave me alone if I asked him to."

"I would have been glad to take care of him for you."

"Thank you. But he promised to leave me alone if I went with him that one last time to take Vanda and Cletis home."

He pulled the wagon to the side of the road and stopped. He turned to her. "Eliza, I don't know what you think of me or if you ever think about me at all. I'm not handsome, and I don't have much worldly goods, but I've loved you ever since the first time you put me in my place." He picked up the reins. "Now I've told you what I've been wanting to, so I guess the rest is up to you."

"Put those down." Eliza waited until he laid the reins back down. "I don't believe you."

He stared at her. "You don't believe me?"

"No, I don't." She crossed her arms. "I know my father paid you to take me to that taffy pull. You didn't want to. Why should I believe anything you say?"

"Because I don't lie."

"Oh, you don't?" Eliza's voice rose. "And what do you call being paid to take a girl out and then acting like you enjoyed it?" She looked at him with accusing eyes. "You kissed me."

James's voice rose in volume to match hers. "I kissed you because I wanted to. And I did enjoy it. Both times." His voice suddenly dropped, and he frowned at her. "What are you talking about being paid, anyway?"

"My father, James." She spoke to him as if he were a child. "Lenny overheard him tell you to take me to Barbara's taffy pull. I would assume that was part of your job."

"Well, it wasn't." He doubled up his fist and hit his knee. "How you and Lenny could have gotten such a fool idea is beyond me. It just so happens that your father knew of my feelings for you."

Eliza's eyes widened as she listened to him.

"I told you I've loved you for a long time. I guess I wasn't too good at hiding it—at least not from your father. When Barbara invited me to her taffy pull, he asked me if I was going and who I would take. I told him I probably wouldn't go because you were the only girl I wanted to take and I didn't think you'd go with me. That day Lenny eavesdropped, your father told me you were in the other shop and would be leaving soon and I should ask you. Again, I told him I didn't think you'd go, but he was insistent that I'd never have a better chance."

He grinned at her then. "I decided it wouldn't hurt to ask. You couldn't do much more than bite my head off, and you'd already done that so many times I was getting used to it."

Eliza sat in stunned silence staring at him. Then she found her voice. "You mean you really wanted to take me? My father didn't talk you into it?"

He nodded, his eyes sparkling with amusement. "I mean I really wanted to take you."

"What about today? Whose idea was it to trick me into going with you?"

He grinned. "That was mine. Your father thought it was a good idea. Who knows? I may get a raise because of it."

"Oh, you." She halfheartedly hit at him, but he caught her hand in his.

They sat, turned toward each other, holding hands. Finally, he said, "I've told you I love you, Eliza. I need to know how you feel about me."

Her eyelids lowered, hiding her eyes. A spot of pink tinged each cheek. "I love you, James."

He moved across the seat closer to her. His forefinger cupped her chin, raising it until she had to look at him. "Please, say that again."

A smile played around the corners of her mouth as she obeyed. "I love you, James."

"Eliza, will you marry me?" James held his breath as he waited for her answer.

She nodded and uttered the one word he wanted to hear. "Yes."

His lips closed on hers in a long, sweet kiss. But when he lifted his head, Eliza's saucy little grin came back. "How much did my father pay you to ask me that?"

He groaned. His tone threatened. "Eliza. . ." But then he stopped and laughed. "I can see right now it'll take a heavy hand to keep you in line."

"And you're just the man for the job?"

He nodded. "That's right, and don't you forget it."

Her eyes widened as James leaned slowly and deliberately toward her. His right arm slipped around her while his left hand touched her cheek, then slid to the back of her head, taking her bonnet with it. When his mouth claimed hers, she felt as if she were floating, and she never wanted to come back to reality.

When the kiss ended, she saw that James was just as shaken as she was. He pulled her close, looking down at her with the light of love still shining in his eyes. "How soon can we get married?"

She pulled her bonnet back up and then leaned back against his shoulder with a sigh. "My birthday is in October. How about then?"

"October!" He pulled forward to see her face better. "I think my birthday would be a better time. It's in June."

"But Kathrene's getting married in June. I don't know if I can get ready that soon."

"Of course you can. What's there to do? We just stand up in front of the church and the preacher talks a little."

Eliza giggled. "Someone had better tell Kathrene she's doing it all wrong, then."

James let out a long breath. "Eliza, we won't need a bunch of stuff. We'll have to live with my mother."

When Eliza didn't say anything, James looked at her. "You

don't want that, do you?"

She smiled, shaking her head. "We need to talk."

"What we need is our own cabin. How long would it take to put together a one-room cabin? A week or two at the most. That's all we'll need, and then after we're married, we'll build on to it. I know the folks around here would help us." He grinned. "We could get married the first of May."

Eliza laughed, then gave him a quick kiss. "You are wonderful, James Hurley. But you're going to lose your job if you don't get these barrels delivered, and then where will we be?"

"You don't have to worry about that." He laughed. "After all, I'm marrying the boss's daughter."

He picked up the reins and flicked them over the horse's back. This time, as the wagon rolled down the country road, there was no distance between its two occupants.

A Letter To Our Readers

Dear Reader:

In order that we might better contribute to your reading enjoyment, we would appreciate your taking a few minutes to respond to the following questions. We welcome your comments and read each form and letter we receive. When completed, please return to the following:

Fiction Editor
Heartsong Presents
PO Box 719
Uhrichsville, Ohio 44683

1. Did you enjoy reading *Eliza* by Mildred Colvin?
   ❏ Very much! I would like to see more books by this author!
   ❏ Moderately. I would have enjoyed it more if

   _____

   _____

   _____

2. Are you a member of **Heartsong Presents**? ❏ Yes ❏ No
   If no, where did you purchase this book? _____

   _____

3. How would you rate, on a scale from 1 (poor) to 5 (superior),
   the cover design? _____

4. On a scale from 1 (poor) to 10 (superior), please rate the
   following elements.

   ____ Heroine   ____ Plot
   ____ Hero   ____ Inspirational theme
   ____ Setting   ____ Secondary characters

5. These characters were special because?_____

_____

_____

6. How has this book inspired your life?_____

_____

_____

7. What settings would you like to see covered in future
Heartsong Presents books? _____

_____

_____

8. What are some inspirational themes you would like to see
treated in future books? _____

_____

_____

9. Would you be interested in reading other **Heartsong
Presents** titles? ❑ Yes ❑ No

10. Please check your age range:
   ❑ Under 18   ❑ 18-24
   ❑ 25-34   ❑ 35-45
   ❑ 46-55   ❑ Over 55

Name_____

Occupation _____

Address_____

City_____ State_____ Zip_____

FRONTIER BRIDES

4 stories in 1

Four romances ride through the sagebrush of yesteryear. Colleen L. Reece shares the compelling stories of people who put their lives on the line to develop a new land. . .and new love.

Historical, paperback, 464 pages, 5 ³/₁₆"x 8"

❤ ❤ ❤ ❤ ❤ ❤ ❤ ❤ ❤ ❤ ❤ ❤ ❤ ❤ ❤ ❤ ❤

❤ ❤ ❤ ❤ ❤ ❤ ❤ ❤ ❤ ❤ ❤ ❤ ❤ ❤ ❤ ❤ ❤ ❤

Heartsong

HEARTSONG PRESENTS TITLES AVAILABLE NOW:

Presents